The Skin
of Our
Teeth

Books by Thornton Wilder

Novels
The Cabala
The Bridge of San Luis Rey
The Woman of Andros
Heaven's My Destination
The Ides of March
The Eighth Day
Theophilus North

Collections of Short Plays
The Angel That Troubled the Waters
The Long Christmas Dinner & Other Plays in One Act

Plays
Our Town
The Merchant of Yonkers
The Skin of Our Teeth
The Matchmaker
The Alcestiad

Essays
American Characteristics & Other Essays
The Journals of Thornton Wilder, 1939–1961

Thornton Wilder

The Skin
of Our
Teeth

A Play

PERENNIAL CLASSICS

Contents

—m—

Foreword by Paula Vogel   vii

The Skin of Our Teeth   3
A play in three acts

Afterword by Tappan Wilder   123

Acknowledgments   154

Foreword

—⁊⁊—

I took my second trip to the MacDowell Colony for artists in 1989.
Two hours, and a world away, outside of Boston, nestled in
time-locked rural roads, stands Peterborough, New Hampshire.
Those of us who are invited to MacDowell remember the hills
and deep forests with gratitude, but we remember the small clus-
tered cottages that house writing desks facing the unpeopled
woods with love.

My second invitation to write among the painters and com-
posers and the poets and fiction writers meant two months of
solitude and solicitude from the colonists and administrators.
On the drive to the colony on the back roads of New Hampshire, I envisioned unpacking my boxes in my cottage, spreading
out my computer and my books, and sitting down to write the
play on domestic violence, *Hot 'n' Throbbing,* upon which I had
spent months of research and preparation.

—Until I actually went to my cottage, that is. The first thing
colonists do, when they are alone in their cottage, is read the
"tombstones" on the wall: wooden tablets that bear the signa-
tures of all the artists who have spent time pacing the cottage

floor. As I traced the names back in time, I saw his signature: Thornton Wilder.

In a fever of excitement, I sat down on my cot and gave myself a pep talk: Vogel, you'd better dig a little deeper this time: you're in *his* cottage. In a night, I scrapped the plans for the play I'd been working on and started page one of another play, *The Baltimore Waltz*. Three weeks later, I emerged, blinking in the sunlight, with a first draft.

For an American dramatist, all roads lead back to Thornton Wilder. Time and again, I return to his scripts and grapple with the problems he tackled—so, it seems, effortlessly—in the unwieldy theatrical apparatus. How do we, when we enter the theater, arrest time and make this art, made of actors and audience, the weight of scenery, flesh and face paint, melt into something fragile? How can we make the material mess of it all—rehearsals, tech, and opening night—disappear into spirit?

The remarkable thing is how we forget, again and again. We forget Wilder's vision and voice; in our memory we assign his works to a nostalgic theater of our youth, encountered first in high school, in community theater, in assigned work judged to be inoffensive enough to constitute the canon for young readers. It's as if he were the theatrical equivalent of castor oil and the honey used to coat the medicinal taste: literature that is good for our moral constitution dredged in sentiment. And then we encounter him on stage as he is and will remain through the ages: tough-minded, exacting, facing the darkness in human existence without apology.

The question I want to face, as prefatory remarks to this edition of *The Skin of Our Teeth*, is why we relegate one of our most remarkable and enduring dramatists to such a place in memory. Because to read him again, whether it be *Our Town, The Skin of Our Teeth*, or his short plays—*The Long Christmas Dinner, Pullman Car Hiawatha*, or *The Happy Journey to Tren-*

ton and Camden—is to be astonished. I am astonished each time I read him, at the force of his work, at the subtle blend of humor and pathos, and his masterful balancing act of abstraction and empathy. I remember anew how much I owe to him, and see in his work the roots or parallels of so many theatrical forebears and influences on my own work: Friedrich Dürrenmatt, Bertolt Brecht, Samuel Beckett, Arthur Miller, Edward Albee, Lanford Wilson, and John Guare.

At one level, the forgetting of Wilder's impact is almost Oedipal—a rejection of the playwright who has given us our American vocabulary, who forged a synthesis of theatrical traditions from the past, from Europe, from Asia—with an American theater taken over by a viral infection of "realism" (an infection from which we've never recovered). By tearing down the walls of the box set, he concentrated our focus on the essential with an almost ruthless insistence that we pay attention to the story of the drama unfolding, rather than the props and decoration, the fussy business of stage machinery inflicted on an audience by the boulevard theater of Broadway.

There is an irony in forgetting the influence of Thornton Wilder. The man who generously paid tribute to James Joyce's *Finnegans Wake* wrote: "I should be very happy if, in the future, some author should feel similarly indebted to any work of mine. Literature has always more resembled a torch race than a furious dispute among heirs." He suffered the charge of plagiarism leveled against *The Skin of Our Teeth,* written in the spirit of tribute to Joyce's work. This spurious charge, brought by Joseph Campbell and Henry Morton Robinson in the two articles they published in late 1942 and early 1943, may well have cost him the Nobel Prize. Of all his contributions to us, Wilder's belief that every new work is in fact a response to the writers who came before, a dialogue between two writers separated in space and time, and not the narcissistic "rip-off" of the imitative, may well be his most important generosity. Wilder may have cast himself in the raiment of others, freely taking from a vast theatrical hope chest, but he always stitched together the old cloth with a new vision and a sense of gratitude.

I have found, in the last three years as I have revisited him on the page, a realization that he was the writer I have borrowed from, not second hand, but third hand—because his work has so imbued the works of writers who have followed him. Wilder has indeed led the torch race, and we remember the recent runner but forget the lead athlete who started the race. There, in *Our Town,* is the bold audience address that I attributed to Tennessee Williams. There, in *The Skin of Our Teeth,* is the collapsing fragile box set exposing the family to the world that I remember in *Death of a Salesman.* There, also in *Skin,* is the nuclear family leaping across centuries and eras that I remember vividly in Caryl Churchill's *Cloud Nine.*

We may also forget Thornton Wilder because he is the last private writer of the twentieth century. After him, any writer of such stature has suffered the glare of celebrity in a culture that consumes us, rather than us consuming culture. Do we remember *Glass Menagerie* more perhaps, because it belongs to the obsessive cult of personality in which the work itself becomes digested by a pop-psych analysis of the writer, Williams? Wilder wrote elegantly about Emily Dickinson, who, while in seclusion, nonetheless embraced the world in her poetry. He managed to draw a parallel veil himself around his own life and was the last writer not subjected to the analytic couch of theater critics. How fascinating that his two towering works, *Our Town* and *The Skin of Our Teeth,* take place in the two locations in American life where there is neither privacy nor acceptance of deviance from the norm—the small town or the suburban tract—places where "almost everybody in the world gets married—you know what I mean? In our town there aren't hardly any exceptions." As a persona in the theater, Wilder successfully evaded the glare of cultural consumption by creating the role of Stage Manager, the character apart from the play-world, the outsider who manipulates the stage, but is not himself captured by the frame of the play-world itself.

Of all his innovations, we are most indebted to the way Wilder transformed the passage of time on stage—an innovation most often attributed to Samuel Beckett a decade later. Wilder wrested theater out of the apocalyptic sense of catastrophe, the ticking of the bomb due to explode in an Aristotelian plot-driven play-world, that had driven all Western drama since the Elizabethans. Instead, in *Our Town* he managed to freeze time, to stop plot, in ways familiar to the Japanese theater and the medieval cycle plays: by staging all moments of time simultaneously so that our awareness of the fragility of time is captured with a delicacy unknown to the American stage of the time. Take, for example, the Stage Manager's introduction of Joe Crowell, the eleven-year-old paperboy in *Our Town:* "Want to tell you something about that boy Joe Crowell there. Joe was awful bright—graduated from high school here, head of his class. So he got a scholarship to Massachusetts Tech. . . . Goin' to be a great engineer, Joe was. But the war broke out and he died in France.—All that education for nothing."

The Skin of Our Teeth was written in the midst of apocalypse, about apocalypse, and here Wilder once again renovates our sense of theatrical time by borrowing a trick from the Viennese playwright Arthur Schnitzler. In order to stop the explosion of the world, he uses a plot structure similar to Schnitzler's *La Ronde:* a pattern plot that creates a cycle. A pattern plot is simply the same act occurring again and again—so that the more furiously our characters run in place, the deeper the rut of stasis. He creates, in *The Skin of Our Teeth,* a theatrical treadmill of entrapment for the Antrobus family, facing the end of time again and again and again, until we realize that the human race is perpetually caught in crises, but also perpetually surviving. The effect of stasis is created by running furiously in the same place, until we end up where we began (the plot form of *The Skin of Our Teeth* would become favored by the French Absurdists, in plays such as *Waiting for Godot* and *Rhinoceros*).

The Skin of Our Teeth was a remarkable gift to an America entrenched in catastrophe, a tribute to the trait of human endurance. But Wilder does not give us a sentimental or easy bromide of a play: the gift for destruction and violence is as innate as our spirit to survive. Remarkably, he suggests that violence begins at home, not abroad in the breasts of our enemies, nor outside the family circle. At the time of the greatest threat, our most American dramatist does not shy away from suggesting we cast out the mote in our own eyes.

I've just seen a remarkable production of the play at Trinity Repertory, in 2002, proving that the text is uncannily timely for an American audience. Why, if *The Skin of Our Teeth* and *Our Town* remain as topical as our daily papers, do we relegate Wilder to a slot for community theater? There is one theatrical element that ages quickly, and is the weakest element among the tricks of our trade: the language. Wilder's use of plot structure remains extraordinary, as do the characters in the Antrobus family and his remarkable use of the stage. But the way people talk on stage has changed under the influence of David Mamet and Quentin Tarantino (themselves influenced by a German writer, Franz Kroetz). The fashionable notion of the "real" in speech right now promotes a view that the way we speak is wounded, incapable of eloquence, or of speaking an original thought. American stage speech right now sounds programmed, reflecting an urban poetry of profanity.

Against the scripts of *American Buffalo* or *Pulp Fiction*, *Fargo* or *The Sopranos*, Wilder's characters speak an American English that sounds quaint to our urban ears: "This is his home . . . conveniently situated near a public school, a Methodist church, and a firehouse; it is right handy to an A. and P.," the announcer says in the first act of *The Skin of Our Teeth*. It sounds quaint, that is, until one drives the back roads of New Hampshire, Massachusetts, or Maine. And probably, the speech sounds "real" when one talks to one's neighbors in any small town, where men still wait until ladies leave the room before spitting out any regionalism not fit for mixed company. Perhaps the reason Wilder is relegated, then, to our community stages is that his characters do not offend the ears of the community.

Regardless of how his characters speak, it is what his characters say that remains timeless. He believed that the most pertinent of voices to listen to in times of crisis are the voices passed down through the ages. If, at this point in time, we may not share Thornton Wilder's confidence in the strength of canonic literature and great minds to pull us through, we can enjoy, in the words of critic Francis Ferguson, Wilder's "marriage of Plato and Groucho Marx."

And now, more than ever, we can appreciate his legacy, his questioning mind and his belief that hope is the most necessary of civic virtues.

—Paula Vogel
Providence, Rhode Island

The Skin

of Our

Teeth

CHARACTERS (in the order of their appearance)

ANNOUNCER
SABINA
MR. FITZPATRICK
MRS. ANTROBUS
DINOSAUR
MAMMOTH
TELEGRAPH BOY
GLADYS
HENRY
MR. ANTROBUS
DOCTOR
PROFESSOR
JUDGE
HOMER

MISS E. MUSE
T. MUSE
MISS M. MUSE
TWO USHERS
TWO DRUM MAJORETTES
FORTUNE TELLER
TWO CHAIR PUSHERS
SIX CONVEENERS
BROADCAST OFFICIAL
DEFEATED CANDIDATE
MR. TREMAYNE
HESTER
IVY
FRED BAILEY

Act I. Home, Excelsior, New Jersey.
Act II. Atlantic City Boardwalk.
Act III. Home, Excelsior, New Jersey.

—◊—

Act I

A projection screen in the middle of the curtain. The first lantern slide: the name of the theatre, and the words: NEWS EVENTS OF THE WORLD. An ANNOUNCER'S *voice is heard.*

ANNOUNCER:

The management takes pleasure in bringing to you—The News Events of the World:

> *Slide of the sun appearing above the horizon.*

Freeport, Long Island.

The sun rose this morning at 6:32 a.m. This gratifying event was first reported by Mrs. Dorothy Stetson of Freeport, Long Island, who promptly telephoned the Mayor.

The Society for Affirming the End of the World at once went into a special session and postponed the arrival of that event for TWENTY-FOUR HOURS.

All honor to Mrs. Stetson for her public spirit.

New York City:

Slide of the front doors of the theatre in which this play is playing; three cleaning WOMEN *with mops and pails.*

The X Theatre. During the daily cleaning of this theatre a number of lost objects were collected as usual by Mesdames Simpson, Pateslewski, and Moriarty.

Among these objects found today was a wedding ring, inscribed: To Eva from Adam. Genesis II:18.

The ring will be restored to the owner or owners, if their credentials are satisfactory.

Tippehatchee, Vermont:

Slide representing a glacier.

The unprecedented cold weather of this summer has produced a condition that has not yet been satisfactorily explained. There is a report that a wall of ice is moving southward across these counties. The disruption of communications by the cold wave now crossing the country has rendered exact information difficult, but little credence is given to the rumor that the ice had pushed the Cathedral of Montreal as far as St. Albans, Vermont.

For further information see your daily papers.

Excelsior, New Jersey:

Slide of a modest suburban home.

The home of Mr. George Antrobus, the inventor of the wheel. The discovery of the wheel, following so closely on the discovery of the lever, has centered the attention of the country on Mr. Antrobus of this attractive suburban residence district. This is his home, a commodious seven-room house, conveniently situated near a public school, a Methodist church, and a firehouse; it is right handy to an A. and P.

Slide of MR. ANTROBUS *on his front steps, smiling and lifting his straw hat. He holds a wheel.*

Mr. Antrobus, himself. He comes of very old stock and has made his way up from next to nothing.

It is reported that he was once a gardener, but left that situation under circumstances that have been variously reported.

Mr. Antrobus is a veteran of foreign wars, and bears a number of scars, front and back.

Slide of MRS. ANTROBUS, *holding some roses.*

This is Mrs. Antrobus, the charming and gracious president of the Excelsior Mothers' Club.

Mrs. Antrobus is an excellent needlewoman; it is she who invented the apron on which so many interesting changes have been rung since.

Slide of the FAMILY *and* SABINA.

Here we see the Antrobuses with their two children, Henry and Gladys, and friend. The friend in the rear is Lily Sabina, the maid.

I know we all want to congratulate this typical American family on its enterprise. We all wish Mr. Antrobus a successful future. Now the management takes you to the interior of this home for a brief visit.

Curtain rises. Living room of a commuter's home. SABINA— *straw-blonde, over-rouged—is standing by the window back center, a feather duster under her elbow.*

SABINA:

Oh, oh, oh! Six o'clock and the master not home yet.

Pray God nothing serious has happened to him crossing the Hudson River. If anything happened to him, we would certainly be inconsolable and have to move into a less desirable residence district.

The fact is I don't know what'll become of us. Here it is the middle of August and the coldest day of the year. It's simply freezing; the dogs are sticking to the sidewalks; can anybody explain that? No.

But I'm not surprised. The whole world's at sixes and sevens, and why the house hasn't fallen down about our ears long ago is a miracle to me.

> *A fragment of the right wall leans precariously over the stage.* SABINA *looks at it nervously and it slowly rights itself.*

Every night this same anxiety as to whether the master will get home safely: whether he'll bring home anything to eat. In the midst of life we are in the midst of death, a truer word was never said.

> *The fragment of scenery flies up into the lofts.* SABINA *is struck dumb with surprise, shrugs her shoulders and starts dusting* MR. ANTROBUS' *chair, including the under side.*

Of course, Mr. Antrobus is a very fine man, an excellent husband and father, a pillar of the church, and has all the best interests of the community at heart. Of course, every muscle goes tight every time he passes a policeman; but what I think is that there are certain charges that ought not to be made, and I think I may add, ought not to be allowed to be made; we're all human; who isn't?

> *She dusts* MRS. ANTROBUS' *rocking chair.*

Mrs. Antrobus is as fine a woman as you could hope to see. She lives only for her children; and if it would be any benefit to her children she'd see the rest of us stretched out dead at her feet without turning a hair,—that's the truth. If you want to know anything more about Mrs. Antrobus, just go and look at a tigress, and look hard.

As to the children—

Well, Henry Antrobus is a real, clean-cut American boy. He'll graduate from High School one of these days, if they make the alphabet any easier.—Henry, when he has a stone in his hand, has a perfect aim; he can hit anything from a bird to an older brother—Oh! I didn't mean to say that!—but it certainly was an unfortunate accident, and it was very hard getting the police out of the house.

Mr. and Mrs. Antrobus' daughter is named Gladys. She'll make some good man a good wife some day, if he'll just come down off the movie screen and ask her.

So here we are!

We've managed to survive for some time now, catch as catch can, the fat and the lean, and if the dinosaurs don't trample us to death, and if the grasshoppers don't eat up our garden, we'll all live to see better days, knock on wood.

Each new child that's born to the Antrobuses seems to them to be sufficient reason for the whole universe's being set in motion; and each new child that dies seems to them to have been spared a whole world of sorrow, and what the end of it will be is still very much an open question.

We've rattled along, hot and cold, for some time now—

A portion of the wall above the door, right, flies up into the air and disappears.

—and my advice to you is not to inquire into why or whither, but just enjoy your ice cream while it's on your plate,—that's my philosophy.

Don't forget that a few years ago we came through the depression by the skin of our teeth! One more tight squeeze like that and where will we be?

This is a cue line. SABINA *looks angrily at the kitchen door and repeats:*

. . . we came through the depression by the skin of our teeth; one more tight squeeze like that and where will we be?

Flustered, she looks through the opening in the right wall; then goes to the window and reopens the Act.

Oh, oh, oh! Six o'clock and the master not home yet. Pray God nothing has happened to him crossing the Hudson. Here it is the middle of August and the coldest day of the year. It's simply freezing; the dogs are sticking. One more tight squeeze like that and where will we be?

VOICE:

Off stage.

Make up something! Invent something!

SABINA:

Well . . . uh . . . this certainly is a fine American home . . . and— uh . . . everybody's very happy . . . and—uh . . .

Suddenly flings pretense to the winds and coming down stage says with indignation:

I can't invent any words for this play, and I'm glad I can't. I hate this play and every word in it.

As for me, I don't understand a single word of it, anyway,—all about the troubles the human race has gone through, there's a subject for you.

Besides, the author hasn't made up his silly mind as to whether we're all living back in caves or in New Jersey today, and that's the way it is all the way through.

Oh—why can't we have plays like we used to have—*Peg o' My Heart,* and *Smilin' Thru,* and *The Bat*—good entertainment with a message you can take home with you?

I took this hateful job because I had to. For two years I've sat up in my room living on a sandwich and a cup of tea a day, waiting for better times in the theatre. And look at me now: I—I who've played *Rain* and *The Barretts of Wimpole Street* and *First Lady*— God in Heaven!

The STAGE MANAGER *puts his head out from the hole in the scenery.*

MR. FITZPATRICK:

Miss Somerset!! Miss Somerset!

SABINA:

Oh! Anyway!—nothing matters! It'll all be the same in a hundred years.

Loudly.

We came through the depression by the skin of our teeth,— that's true!—one more tight squeeze like that and where will we be?

Enter MRS. ANTROBUS, *a mother.*

MRS. ANTROBUS:

Sabina, you've let the fire go out.

SABINA:

In a lather.

One-thing-and-another; don't-know-whether-my-wits-are-upside-or-down; might-as-well-be-dead-as-alive-in-a-house-all-sixes-and-sevens. . . .

MRS. ANTROBUS:

You've let the fire go out. Here it is the coldest day of the year right in the middle of August, and you've let the fire go out.

SABINA:

Mrs. Antrobus, I'd like to give my two weeks' notice, Mrs. Antrobus. A girl like I can get a situation in a home where they're rich enough to have a fire in every room, Mrs. Antrobus, and a girl don't have to carry the responsibility of the whole house on her two shoulders. And a home without children, Mrs. Antrobus, because children are a thing only a parent can stand, and a truer word was never said; and a home, Mrs. Antrobus, where the master of the house don't pinch decent, self-respecting girls when he meets them in a dark corridor. I mention no names and make no charges. So you have my notice, Mrs. Antrobus. I hope that's perfectly clear.

MRS. ANTROBUS:

You've let the fire go out!—Have you milked the mammoth?

SABINA:

I don't understand a word of this play.—Yes, I've milked the mammoth.

MRS. ANTROBUS:

Until Mr. Antrobus comes home we have no food and we have no fire. You'd better go over to the neighbors and borrow some fire.

SABINA:

Mrs. Antrobus! I can't! I'd die on the way, you know I would. It's worse than January. The dogs are sticking to the sidewalks. I'd die.

MRS. ANTROBUS:

Very well, I'll go.

SABINA:

Even more distraught, coming forward and sinking on her knees.

You'd never come back alive; we'd all perish; if you weren't here, we'd just perish. How do we know Mr. Antrobus'll be back? We don't know. If you go out, I'll just kill myself.

MRS. ANTROBUS:

Get up, Sabina.

SABINA:

Every night it's the same thing. Will he come back safe, or won't he? Will we starve to death, or freeze to death, or boil to death or will we be killed by burglars? I don't know why we go on living. I don't know why we go on living at all. It's easier being dead.

She flings her arms on the table and buries her head in them. In each of the succeeding speeches she flings her head up—and sometimes her hands—then quickly buries her head again.

MRS. ANTROBUS:

The same thing! Always throwing up the sponge, Sabina. Always announcing your own death. But give you a new hat—or a plate of ice cream—or a ticket to the movies, and you want to live forever.

SABINA:

You don't care whether we live or die; all you care about is those children. If it would be any benefit to them you'd be glad to see us all stretched out dead.

MRS. ANTROBUS:

Well, maybe I would.

SABINA:

And what do they care about? Themselves—that's all they care about.

Shrilly.

They make fun of you behind your back. Don't tell me: they're ashamed of you. Half the time, they pretend they're someone else's children. Little thanks you get from them.

MRS. ANTROBUS:

I'm not asking for any thanks.

SABINA:

And Mr. Antrobus—you don't understand *him*. All that work he does—trying to discover the alphabet and the multiplication table. Whenever he tries to learn anything you fight against it.

MRS. ANTROBUS:

Oh, Sabina, I know you.

When Mr. Antrobus raped you home from your Sabine hills, he did it to insult me.

He did it for your pretty face, and to insult me.

You were the new wife, weren't you?

For a year or two you lay on your bed all day and polished the nails on your hands and feet.

You made puff-balls of the combings of your hair and you blew them up to the ceiling.

And I washed your underclothes and I made you chicken broths.

I bore children and between my very groans I stirred the cream that you'd put on your face.

But I knew you wouldn't last.

You didn't last.

SABINA:

But it was I who encouraged Mr. Antrobus to make the alphabet. I'm sorry to say it, Mrs. Antrobus, but you're not a beautiful woman, and you can never know what a man could do if he tried. It's girls like I who inspire the multiplication table.

I'm sorry to say it, but you're not a beautiful woman, Mrs. Antrobus, and that's the God's truth.

MRS. ANTROBUS:

And you didn't last—you sank to the kitchen. And what do you do there? *You let the fire go out!*

No wonder to you it seems easier being dead.

Reading and writing and counting on your fingers is all very well in their way,—but I keep the home going.

MRS. ANTROBUS:

—There's that dinosaur on the front lawn again.—Shoo! Go away. Go away.

The baby DINOSAUR *puts his head in the window.*

DINOSAUR:

It's cold.

MRS. ANTROBUS:

You go around to the back of the house where you belong.

DINOSAUR:

It's cold.

The DINOSAUR *disappears.* MRS. ANTROBUS *goes calmly out.*

SABINA *slowly raises her head and speaks to the audience. The central portion of the center wall rises, pauses, and disappears into the loft.*

SABINA:

Now that you audience are listening to this, too, I understand it a little better.

I wish eleven o'clock were here; I don't want to be dragged through this whole play again.

The TELEGRAPH BOY *is seen entering along the back wall of the stage from the right. She catches sight of him and calls:*

Mrs. Antrobus! Mrs. Antrobus! Help! There's a strange man coming to the house. He's coming up the walk, help!

Enter MRS. ANTROBUS *in alarm, but efficient.*

MRS. ANTROBUS:

Help me quick!

They barricade the door by piling the furniture against it.

Who is it? What do you want?

TELEGRAPH BOY:

A telegram for Mrs. Antrobus from Mr. Antrobus in the city.

SABINA:

Are you sure, are you sure? Maybe it's just a trap!

MRS. ANTROBUS:

I know his voice, Sabina. We can open the door.

Enter the TELEGRAPH BOY, *12 years old, in uniform. The* DINOSAUR *and* MAMMOTH *slip by him into the room and settle down front right.*

I'm sorry we kept you waiting. We have to be careful, you know.

To the ANIMALS.

Hm! . . . Will you be quiet?

They nod.

Have you had your supper?

They nod.

Are you *ready* to come in?

They nod.

Young man, have you any fire with you? Then light the grate, will you?

He nods, produces something like a briquet; and kneels by the imagined fireplace, footlights center. Pause.

What are people saying about this cold weather?

He makes a doubtful shrug with his shoulders.

Sabina, take this stick and go and light the stove.

SABINA:

Like I told you, Mrs. Antrobus; two weeks. That's the law. I hope that's perfectly clear.

Exit.

MRS. ANTROBUS:

What about this cold weather?

TELEGRAPH BOY:

Lowered eyes.

Of course, I don't know anything . . . but they say there's a wall of ice moving down from the North, that's what they say. We can't get Boston by telegraph, and they're burning pianos in Hartford.

. . . It moves everything in front of it, churches and post offices and city halls.

I live in Brooklyn myself.

MRS. ANTROBUS:

What are people doing about it?

TELEGRAPH BOY:

Well . . . uh . . . Talking, mostly.

Or just what you'd do a day in February.

There are some that are trying to go South and the roads are crowded; but you can't take old people and children very far in a cold like this.

MRS. ANTROBUS:

—What's this telegram you have for me?

TELEGRAPH BOY:

Fingertips to his forehead.

If you wait just a minute; I've got to remember it.

The ANIMALS *have left their corner and are nosing him. Presently they take places on either side of him, leaning against his hips, like heraldic beasts.*

This telegram was flashed from Murray Hill to University Heights! And then by puffs of smoke from University Heights to Staten Island.

And then by lantern from Staten Island to Plainfield, New Jersey. What hath God wrought!

He clears his throat.

"To Mrs. Antrobus, Excelsior, New Jersey:

My dear wife, will be an hour late. Busy day at the office. Don't worry the children about the cold just keep them warm burn everything except Shakespeare."

Pause.

MRS. ANTROBUS:

Men!—He knows I'd burn ten Shakespeares to prevent a child of mine from having one cold in the head. What does it say next?

Enter SABINA.

TELEGRAPH BOY:

"Have made great discoveries today have separated em from en."

SABINA:

I know what that is, that's the alphabet, yes it is. Mr. Antrobus is just the cleverest man. Why, when the alphabet's finished, we'll be able to tell the future and everything.

TELEGRAPH BOY:

Then listen to this: "Ten tens make a hundred semi-colon consequences far-reaching."

Watches for effect.

MRS. ANTROBUS:

The earth's turning to ice, and all he can do is to make up new numbers.

TELEGRAPH BOY:

Well, Mrs. Antrobus, like the head man at our office said: a few more discoveries like that and we'll be worth freezing.

MRS. ANTROBUS:

What does he say next?

TELEGRAPH BOY:

I . . . I can't do this last part very well.

He clears his throat and sings.

"Happy w'dding ann'vers'ry to you, Happy ann'vers'ry to you—"

The ANIMALS *begin to howl soulfully;* SABINA *screams with pleasure.*

MRS. ANTROBUS:

Dolly! Frederick! Be quiet.

TELEGRAPH BOY:

Above the din.

"Happy w'dding ann'vers'ry, dear Eva; happy w'dding ann'vers'ry to you."

MRS. ANTROBUS:

Is that in the telegram? Are they singing telegrams now?

He nods.

The earth's getting so silly no wonder the sun turns cold.

SABINA:

Mrs. Antrobus, I want to take back the notice I gave you. Mrs. Antrobus, I don't want to leave a house that gets such interesting telegrams and I'm sorry for anything I said. I really am.

MRS. ANTROBUS:

Young man, I'd like to give you something for all this trouble;
Mr. Antrobus isn't home yet and I have no money and no food
in the house—

TELEGRAPH BOY:

Mrs. Antrobus . . . I don't like to . . . appear to . . . ask for anything, but . . .

MRS. ANTROBUS:

What is it you'd like?

TELEGRAPH BOY:

Do you happen to have an old needle you could spare? My wife
just sits home all day thinking about needles.

SABINA:

Shrilly.

We only got two in the house. Mrs. Antrobus, you know we only
got two in the house.

MRS. ANTROBUS:

After a look at SABINA *taking a needle from her collar.*

Why yes, I can spare this.

TELEGRAPH BOY:

Lowered eyes.

Thank you, Mrs. Antrobus. Mrs. Antrobus, can I ask you something else? I have two sons of my own; if the cold gets worse,
what should I do?

SABINA:

I think we'll all perish, that's what I think. Cold like this in
August is just the end of the whole world.

Silence.

MRS. ANTROBUS:

I don't know. After all, what does one do about anything? Just keep as warm as you can. And don't let your wife and children see that you're worried.

TELEGRAPH BOY:

Yes. . . . Thank you, Mrs. Antrobus. Well, I'd better be going.— Oh, I forgot! There's one more sentence in the telegram. "Three cheers have invented the wheel."

MRS. ANTROBUS:

A wheel? What's a wheel?

TELEGRAPH BOY:

I don't know. That's what it said. The sign for it is like this. Well, goodbye.

The WOMEN *see him to the door, with goodbyes and injunctions to keep warm.*

SABINA:

Apron to her eyes, wailing.

Mrs. Antrobus, it looks to me like all the nice men in the world are already married; I don't know why that is.

Exit.

MRS. ANTROBUS:

Thoughtful; to the ANIMALS.

Do you ever remember hearing tell of any cold like this in August?

The ANIMALS *shake their heads.*

From your grandmothers or anyone?

They shake their heads.

Have you any suggestions?

They shake their heads.

She pulls her shawl around, goes to the front door and opening it an inch calls:

HENRY. GLADYS. CHILDREN. Come right in and get warm. No, no, when mama says a thing she means it.

Henry! HENRY. Put down that stone. You know what happened last time.

Shriek.

HENRY! Put down that stone!

Gladys! Put down your dress!! Try and be a lady.

The CHILDREN *bound in and dash to the fire. They take off their winter things and leave them in heaps on the floor.*

GLADYS:
Mama, I'm hungry. Mama, why is it so cold?

HENRY:
At the same time.

Mama, why doesn't it snow? Mama, when's supper ready?

Maybe, it'll snow and we can make snowballs.

GLADYS:
Mama, it's so cold that in one more minute I just couldn't of stood it.

MRS. ANTROBUS:
Settle down, both of you, I want to talk to you.

She draws up a hassock and sits front center over the orchestra pit before the imaginary fire. The CHILDREN *stretch out on the floor, leaning against her lap. Tableau by Raphael. The* ANIMALS *edge up and complete the triangle.*

It's just a cold spell of some kind. Now listen to what I'm saying:

When your father comes home I want you to be extra quiet.

He's had a hard day at the office and I don't know but what he may have one of his moods.

I just got a telegram from him very happy and excited, and you know what that means. Your father's temper's uneven; I guess you know that.

Shriek.

Henry! Henry!

Why—why can't you remember to keep your hair down over your forehead? You must keep that scar covered up. Don't you know that when your father sees it he loses all control over himself? He goes crazy. He wants to die.

After a moment's despair she collects herself decisively, wets the hem of her apron in her mouth and starts polishing his forehead vigorously.

Lift your head up. Stop squirming. Blessed me, sometimes I think that it's going away—and then there it is: just as red as ever.

HENRY:
Mama, today at school two teachers forgot and called me by my old name. They forgot, Mama. You'd better write another letter to the principal, so that he'll tell them I've changed my name. Right out in class they called me: Cain.

MRS. ANTROBUS:

Putting her hand on his mouth, too late; hoarsely.

Don't say it.

Polishing feverishly.

If you're good they'll forget it. Henry, you didn't hit anyone . . . today, did you?

HENRY:

Oh . . . no-o-o!

MRS. ANTROBUS:

Still working, not looking at Gladys.

And, Gladys, I want you to be especially nice to your father to-night. You know what he calls you when you're good—his little angel, his little star. Keep your dress down like a little lady. And keep your voice nice and low. Gladys Antrobus!! What's that red stuff you have on your face?

Slaps her.

You're a filthy detestable child!

Rises in real, though temporary, repudiation and despair.

Get away from me, both of you! I wish I'd never seen sight or sound of you. Let the cold come! I can't stand it. I don't want to go on.

She walks away.

GLADYS:

Weeping.

All the girls at school do, Mama.

MRS. ANTROBUS:

Shrieking.

I'm through with you, that's all!—Sabina! Sabina!—Don't you know your father'd go crazy if he saw that paint on your face? Don't you know your father thinks you're perfect? Don't you know he couldn't live if he didn't think you were perfect?— Sabina!

Enter SABINA.

SABINA:
Yes, Mrs. Antrobus!

MRS. ANTROBUS:
Take this girl out into the kitchen and wash her face with the scrubbing brush.

MR. ANTROBUS:
Outside, roaring.

"I've been working on the railroad, all the livelong day . . . etc."

The ANIMALS *start running around in circles, bellowing.* SABINA *rushes to the window.*

MRS. ANTROBUS:
Sabina, what's that noise outside?

SABINA:
Oh, it's a drunken tramp. It's a giant, Mrs. Antrobus. We'll all be killed in our beds, I know it!

MRS. ANTROBUS:
Help me quick. Quick. Everybody.

Again they stack all the furniture against the door. MR. ANTROBUS *pounds and bellows.*

Who is it? What do you want?—Sabina, have you any boiling water ready?—Who is it?

MR. ANTROBUS:

Broken-down camel of a pig's snout, open this door.

MRS. ANTROBUS:

God be praised! It's your father.—Just a minute, George!— Sabina, clear the door, quick. Gladys, come here while I clean your nasty face!

MR. ANTROBUS:

She-bitch of a goat's gizzard, I'll break every bone in your body. Let me in or I'll tear the whole house down.

MRS. ANTROBUS:

Just a minute, George, something's the matter with the lock.

MR. ANTROBUS:

Open the door or I'll tear your livers out. I'll smash your brains on the ceiling, and Devil take the hindmost.

MRS. ANTROBUS:

Now, you can open the door, Sabina. I'm ready.

The door is flung open. Silence. MR. ANTROBUS—*face of a Keystone Comedy Cop—stands there in fur cap and blanket. His arms are full of parcels, including a large stone wheel with a center in it. One hand carries a railroad man's lantern. Suddenly he bursts into joyous roar.*

MR. ANTROBUS:

Well, how's the whole crooked family?

Relief. Laughter. Tears. Jumping up and down. ANIMALS *cavorting.* ANTROBUS *throws the parcels on the ground. Hurls his cap and blanket after them. Heroic embraces. Melee of* HUMANS *and* ANIMALS, SABINA *included.*

I'll be scalded and tarred if a man can't get a little welcome when he comes home. Well, Maggie, you old gunny-sack, how's the broken down old weather hen?—Sabina, old fishbait, old skunkpot.—And the children,—how've the little smellers been?

GLADYS:

Papa, Papa, Papa, Papa, Papa.

MR. ANTROBUS:

How've they been, Maggie?

MRS. ANTROBUS:

Well, I must say, they've been as good as gold. I haven't had to raise my voice once. I don't know what's the matter with them.

ANTROBUS:

Kneeling before GLADYS.

Papa's little weasel, eh?—Sabina, there's some food for you.— Papa's little gopher?

GLADYS:

Her arm around his neck.

Papa, you're always teasing me.

ANTROBUS:

And Henry? Nothing rash today, I hope. Nothing rash?

HENRY:

No, Papa.

ANTROBUS:

Roaring.

Well that's good, that's good—I'll bet Sabina let the fire go out.

SABINA:

Mr. Antrobus, I've given my notice. I'm leaving two weeks from today. I'm sorry, but I'm leaving.

ANTROBUS:

Roar.

Well, if you leave now you'll freeze to death, so go and cook the dinner.

SABINA:

Two weeks, that's the law.

Exit.

ANTROBUS:

Did you get my telegram?

MRS. ANTROBUS:

Yes.—What's a wheel?

He indicates the wheel with a glance. HENRY *is rolling it around the floor. Rapid, hoarse interchange:* MRS. ANTROBUS: *What does this cold weather mean? It's below freezing.* ANTROBUS: *Not before the children!* MRS. ANTROBUS: *Shouldn't we do something about it?—start off, move?* ANTROBUS: *Not before the children!!! He gives* HENRY *a sharp slap.*

HENRY:

Papa, you hit me!

ANTROBUS:

Well, remember it. That's to make you remember today. Today. The day the alphabet's finished; and the day that we *saw* the hundred—the hundred, the hundred, the hundred, the hundred, the hundred—there's no end to 'em.

I've had a day at the office!

Take a look at that wheel, Maggie—when I've got that to rights: you'll see a sight.

There's a reward there for all the walking you've done.

MRS. ANTROBUS:

How do you mean?

ANTROBUS:

On the hassock looking into the fire; with awe.

Maggie, we've reached the top of the wave. There's not much more to be done. We're there!

MRS. ANTROBUS:

Cutting across his mood sharply.

And the ice?

ANTROBUS:

The ice!

HENRY:

Playing with the wheel.

Papa, you could put a chair on this.

ANTROBUS:

Broodingly.

Ye-e-s, any booby can fool with it now,—but I thought of it first.

MRS. ANTROBUS:

Children, go out in the kitchen. I want to talk to your father alone.

The CHILDREN *go out.*

ANTROBUS *has moved to his chair up left. He takes the goldfish bowl on his lap; pulls the canary cage down to the level of his face. Both the* ANIMALS *put their paws up on the arm of his chair.* MRS. ANTROBUS *faces him across the room, like a judge.*

MRS. ANTROBUS:

Well?

ANTROBUS:

Shortly.

It's cold.—How things been, eh? Keck, keck, keck.—And you, Millicent?

MRS. ANTROBUS:

I know it's cold.

ANTROBUS:

To the canary.

No spilling of sunflower seed, eh? No singing after lights-out, y'know what I mean?

MRS. ANTROBUS:

You can try and prevent us freezing to death, can't you? You can do something? We can start moving. Or we can go on the animals' backs?

ANTROBUS:

The best thing about animals is that they don't talk much.

MAMMOTH:

It's cold.

ANTROBUS:

Eh, eh, eh! Watch that!—

—By midnight we'd turn to ice. The roads are full of people now who can scarcely lift a foot from the ground. The grass out in front is like iron,—which reminds me, I have another needle for you.—The people up north—where are they?

Frozen . . . crushed . . . .

MRS. ANTROBUS:

Is that what's going to happen to us?—Will you answer me?

ANTROBUS:

I don't know. I don't know anything. Some say that the ice is going slower. Some say that it's stopped. The sun's growing cold. What can I do about that? Nothing we can do but burn everything in the house, and the fenceposts and the barn. Keep the fire going. When we have no more fire, we die.

MRS. ANTROBUS:

Well, why didn't you say so in the first place?

MRS. ANTROBUS *is about to march off when she catches sight of two* REFUGEES, *men, who have appeared against the back wall of the theatre and who are soon joined by others.*

REFUGEES:

Mr. Antrobus! Mr. Antrobus! Mr. An-nn-tro-bus!

MRS. ANTROBUS:

Who's that? Who's that calling you?

ANTROBUS:

Clearing his throat guiltily.

Hm—let me see.

Two REFUGEES *come up to the window.*

REFUGEE:

Could we warm our hands for a moment, Mr. Antrobus. It's very cold, Mr. Antrobus.

ANOTHER REFUGEE:

Mr. Antrobus, I wonder if you have a piece of bread or something that you could spare.

Silence. They wait humbly. MRS. ANTROBUS *stands rooted to the spot. Suddenly a knock at the door, then another hand knocking in short rapid blows.*

MRS. ANTROBUS:

Who are these people? Why, they're all over the front yard.

What have they come *here* for?

Enter SABINA.

SABINA:

Mrs. Antrobus! There are some tramps knocking at the back door.

MRS. ANTROBUS:

George, tell these people to go away. Tell them to move right along. I'll go and send them away from the back door. Sabina, come with me.

She goes out energetically.

ANTROBUS:

Sabina! Stay here! I have something to say to you.

He goes to the door and opens it a crack and talks through it.

Ladies and gentlemen! I'll have to ask you to wait a few minutes longer. It'll be all right . . . while you're waiting you might each one pull up a stake of the fence. We'll need them all for the fireplace. There'll be coffee and sandwiches in a moment.

SABINA *looks out door over his shoulder and suddenly extends her arm pointing, with a scream.*

SABINA:

Mr. Antrobus, what's that??—that big white thing? Mr. Antrobus, it's ICE. It's ICE!!

ANTROBUS:

Sabina, I want you to go in the kitchen and make a lot of coffee. Make a whole pail full.

SABINA:

Pail full!!

ANTROBUS:

With gesture.

And sandwiches . . . piles of them . . . like this.

SABINA:

Mr. An . . . !!

Suddenly she drops the play, and says in her own person as MISS SOMERSET, *with surprise.*

Oh, *I* see what this part of the play means now! This means refugees.

She starts to cross to the proscenium.

Oh, I don't like it. I don't like it.

She leans against the proscenium and bursts into tears.

ANTROBUS:

Miss Somerset!

Voice of the STAGE MANAGER.

Miss Somerset!

SABINA:

Energetically, to the audience.

Ladies and gentlemen! Don't take this play serious. The world's not coming to an end. You know it's not. People exaggerate! Most people really have enough to eat and a roof over their heads. Nobody actually starves—you can always eat grass or something. That ice-business—why, it was a long, long time ago. Besides they were only savages. Savages don't love their families—not like we do.

ANTROBUS *and* STAGE MANAGER:

Miss Somerset!!

There is renewed knocking at the door.

SABINA:

All right. I'll say the lines, but I won't think about the play.

Enter MRS. ANTROBUS.

SABINA:

Parting thrust at the audience.

And I advise *you* not to think about the play, either.

Exit SABINA.

MRS. ANTROBUS:

George, these tramps say that you asked them to come to the house. What does this mean?

Knocking at the door.

ANTROBUS:

Just . . . uh . . . .There are a few friends, Maggie, I met on the road. Real nice, real useful people. . . .

MRS. ANTROBUS:

Back to the door.

Now, don't you ask them in!

George Antrobus, not another soul comes in here over my dead body.

ANTROBUS:

Maggie, there's a doctor there. Never hurts to have a good doctor in the house. We've lost a peck of children, one way and another. You can never tell when a child's throat will get stopped up. What you and I have seen—!!!

He puts his fingers on his throat, and imitates diphtheria.

MRS. ANTROBUS:

Well, just one person then, the Doctor. The others can go right along the road.

ANTROBUS:

Maggie, there's an old man, particular friend of mine—

MRS. ANTROBUS:

I won't listen to you—

ANTROBUS:

It was he that really started off the A.B.C.'s.

MRS. ANTROBUS:

I don't care if he perishes. We can do without reading or writing. We can't do without food.

ANTROBUS:

Then let the ice come!! Drink your coffee!! I don't want any coffee if I can't drink it with some good people.

MRS. ANTROBUS:

Stop shouting. Who else is there trying to push us off the cliff?

ANTROBUS:

Well, there's the man . . . who makes all the laws. Judge Moses!

MRS. ANTROBUS:

Judges can't help us now.

ANTROBUS:

And if the ice melts? . . . and if we pull through? Have you and I been able to bring up Henry? What have we done?

MRS. ANTROBUS:

Who are those old women?

ANTROBUS:

Coughs.

Up in town there are nine sisters. There are three or four of them here. They're sort of music teachers . . . and one of them recites and one of them—

MRS. ANTROBUS:

That's the end. A singing troupe! Well, take your choice, live or die. Starve your own children before your face.

ANTROBUS:

Gently.

These people don't take much. They're used to starving.

They'll sleep on the floor.

Besides, Maggie, listen: no, listen:

Who've we got in the house, but Sabina? Sabina's always afraid the worst will happen. Whose spirits can she keep up? Maggie, these people never give up. They think they'll live and work forever.

MRS. ANTROBUS:

Walks slowly to the middle of the room.

All right, let them in. Let them in. You're master here.

Softly.

—But these animals must go. Enough's enough. They'll soon be big enough to push the walls down, anyway. Take them away.

ANTROBUS:

Sadly.

All right. The dinosaur and mammoth—! Come on, baby, come on Frederick. Come for a walk. That's a good little fellow.

DINOSAUR:

It's cold.

ANTROBUS:

Yes, nice cold fresh air. Bracing.

> *He holds the door open and the* ANIMALS *go out. He beckons to his friends. The* REFUGEES *are typical elderly out-of-works from the streets of New York today.* JUDGE MOSES *wears a skull cap.* HOMER *is a blind beggar with a guitar. The seedy crowd shuffles in and waits humbly and expectantly.* ANTROBUS *introduces them to his wife who bows to each with a stately bend of her head.*

Make yourself at home, Maggie, this the doctor . . . m . . . Coffee'll be here in a minute. . . . Professor, this is my wife. . . . And: . . . Judge . . . Maggie, you know the Judge.

An old blind man with a guitar.

Maggie, you know . . . you know Homer?—Come right in, Judge.—

Miss Muse—are some of your sisters here? Come right in. . . . Miss E. Muse; Miss T. Muse, Miss M. Muse.

MRS. ANTROBUS:

Pleased to meet you.

Just . . . make yourself comfortable. Supper'll be ready in a minute.

She goes out, abruptly.

ANTROBUS:
Make yourself at home, friends. I'll be right back.

He goes out.

The REFUGEES *stare about them in awe. Presently several voices start whispering "Homer! Homer!" All take it up.* HOMER *strikes a chord or two on his guitar, then starts to speak:*

HOMER:
Μῆνιν ἄειδε, θεά, Πηληϊάδεω Ἀχιλῆος,
οὐλομένην, ἥ μυρί᾽ Ἀχαιοῖς ἄλγε᾽ ἔθηκεν,
πολλὰς δ᾽ ἰφθίμους ψυχὰς—

HOMER'S *face shows he is lost in thought and memory and the words die away on his lips. The* REFUGEES *likewise nod in dreamy recollection. Soon the whisper "Moses, Moses!" goes around. An aged Jew parts his heard and recites dramatically:*

MOSES:
בְּרֵאשִׁית בָּרָא אֱלֹהִים אֵת הַשָּׁמַיִם וְאֵת הָאָרֶץ׃ וְהָאָרֶץ הָיְתָה תֹהוּ
וָבֹהוּ וְחֹשֶׁךְ עַל־פְּנֵי תְהוֹם וְרוּחַ אֱלֹהִים מְרַחֶפֶת עַל־פְּנֵי הַמָּיִם׃

The same dying away of the words take place, and on the part of the REFUGEES *the same retreat into recollection. Some of them murmur, "Yes, yes."*

The mood is broken by the abrupt entrance of MR. *and* MRS. ANTROBUS *and* SABINA *bearing platters of sandwiches and a pail of coffee.* SABINA *stops and stares at the guests.*

MR. ANTROBUS:
Sabina, pass the sandwiches.

SABINA:

I thought I was working in a respectable house that had respectable guests. I'm giving my notice, Mr. Antrobus: two weeks, that's the law.

MR. ANTROBUS:

Sabina! Pass the sandwiches.

SABINA:

Two weeks, that's the law.

MR. ANTROBUS:

There's the law. That's Moses.

SABINA:

Stares.

The Ten Commandments—FAUGH!!—(*To Audience*)

That's the worst line I've ever had to say on any stage.

ANTROBUS:

I think the best thing to do is just not to stand on ceremony, but pass the sandwiches around from left to right—Judge, help yourself to one of these.

MRS. ANTROBUS:

The roads are crowded, I hear?

THE GUESTS:

All talking at once.

Oh, ma'am, you can't imagine. . . . You can hardly put one foot before you . . . people are trampling one another.

Sudden silence.

MRS. ANTROBUS:

Well, you know what I think it is,—I think it's sun-spots!

THE GUESTS:
Discreet hubbub.

Oh, you're right, Mrs. Antrobus . . . that's what it is. . . . That's what I was saying the other day.

Sudden silence.

ANTROBUS:
Well, I don't believe the whole world's going to turn to ice.

All eyes are fixed on him, waiting.

I can't believe it. Judge! Have we worked for nothing? Professor! Have we just failed in the whole thing?

MRS. ANTROBUS:
It is certainly very strange—well fortunately on both sides of the family we come of very hearty stock.—Doctor, I want you to meet my children. They're eating their supper now. And of course I want them to meet you.

MISS M. MUSE:
How many children have you, Mrs. Antrobus?

MRS. ANTROBUS:
I have two,—a boy and a girl.

MOSES:
Softly.

I understood you had two sons, Mrs. Antrobus.

MRS. ANTROBUS *in blind suffering; she walks toward the foot lights.*

MRS. ANTROBUS:
In a low voice.

Abel, Abel, my son, my son, Abel, my son, Abel, Abel, my son.

The REFUGEES *move with few steps toward her as though in comfort murmuring words in Greek, Hebrew, German, et cetera.*

A piercing shriek from the kitchen,—SABINA'S *voice.*

All heads turn.

ANTROBUS:

What's that?

SABINA *enters, bursting with indignation, pulling on her gloves.*

SABINA:

Mr. Antrobus—that son of yours, that boy Henry Antrobus—I don't stay in this house another moment!—He's not fit to live among respectable folks and that's a fact.

MRS. ANTROBUS:

Don't say another word, Sabina. I'll be right back.

Without waiting for an answer she goes past her into the kitchen.

SABINA:

Mr. Antrobus, Henry has thrown a stone again and if he hasn't killed the boy that lives next door, I'm very much mistaken. He finished his supper and went out to play; and I heard such a fight; and then I saw it. I saw it with my own eyes. And it looked to me like stark murder.

MRS. ANTROBUS *appears at the kitchen door, shielding* HENRY *who follows her. When she steps aside, we see on* HENRY'S *forehead a large ochre and scarlet scar in the shape of a* C. MR. ANTROBUS *starts toward him. A pause.* HENRY *is heard saying under his breath:*

HENRY:

He was going to take the wheel away from me. He started to throw a stone at me first.

MRS. ANTROBUS:

George, it was just a boyish impulse. Remember how young he is.

Louder, in an urgent wail.

George, he's only four thousand years old.

SABINA:

And everything was going along so nicely!

Silence. ANTROBUS *goes back to the fireplace.*

ANTROBUS:

Put out the fire! Put out all the fires.

Violently.

No wonder the sun grows cold.

He starts stamping on the fireplace.

MRS. ANTROBUS:

Doctor! Judge! Help me!—George, have you lost your mind?

ANTROBUS:

There is no mind. We'll not try to live.

To the guests.

Give it up. Give up trying.

MRS. ANTROBUS *seizes him.*

SABINA:

Mr. Antrobus! I'm downright ashamed of you.

MRS. ANTROBUS:

George, have some more coffee.—Gladys! Where's Gladys gone?

GLADYS *steps in, frightened.*

GLADYS:

Here I am, mama.

MRS. ANTROBUS:

Go upstairs and bring your father's slippers. How could you forget a thing like that, when you know how tired he is?

ANTROBUS *sits in his chair. He covers his face with his hands.* MRS. ANTROBUS *turns to the* REFUGEES:

Can't some of you sing? It's your business in life to sing, isn't it? Sabina!

Several of the women clear their throats tentatively, and with frightened faces gather around HOMER'S *guitar. He establishes a few chords. Almost inaudibly they start singing, led by* SABINA: "Jingle Bells." MRS. ANTROBUS *continues to* ANTROBUS *in a low voice, while taking off his shoes:*

George, remember all the other times. When the volcanoes came right up in the front yard.

And the time the grasshoppers ate every single leaf and blade of grass, and all the grain and spinach you'd grown with your own hands. And the summer there were earthquakes every night.

ANTROBUS:

Henry! Henry!

Puts his hand on his forehead.

Myself. All of us, we're covered with blood.

MRS. ANTROBUS:

Then remember all the times you were pleased with him and when you were proud of yourself.—Henry! Henry! Come here and recite to your father the multiplication table that you do so nicely.

HENRY *kneels on one knee beside his father and starts whispering the multiplication table.*

HENRY:
Finally.

Two times six is twelve; three times six is eighteen—I don't think I know the sixes.

Enter GLADYS *with the slippers.* MRS. ANTROBUS *makes stern gestures to her: Go in there and do your best. The* GUESTS *are now singing "Tenting Tonight."*

GLADYS:
Putting slippers on his feet.

Papa . . . papa . . . I was very good in school today. Miss Conover said right out in class that if all the girls had as good manners as Gladys Antrobus, that the world would be a very different place to live in.

MRS. ANTROBUS:
You recited a piece at assembly, didn't you? Recite it to your father.

GLADYS:
Papa, do you want to hear what I recited in class?

Fierce directorial glance from her mother.

"THE STAR" by Henry Wadsworth LONGFELLOW.

MRS. ANTROBUS:
Wait!!! The fire's going out. There isn't enough wood!

Henry, go upstairs and bring down the chairs and start breaking up the beds.

Exit HENRY. *The singers return to "Jingle Bells," still very softly.*

GLADYS:

Look, Papa, here's my report card. Lookit. Conduct A! Look, Papa. Papa, do you want to hear the Star, by Henry Wadsworth Longfellow? Papa, you're not mad at me, are you?—I know it'll get warmer. Soon it'll be just like spring, and we can go to a picnic at the Hibernian Picnic Grounds like you always like to do, don't you remember? Papa, just look at me once.

Enter HENRY *with some chairs.*

ANTROBUS:

You recited in assembly, did you?

She nods eagerly.

You didn't forget it?

GLADYS:

No!!! I was perfect.

Pause. Then ANTROBUS *rises, goes to the front door and opens it. The* REFUGEES *draw back timidly; the song stops; he peers out of the door, then closes it.*

ANTROBUS:

With decision, suddenly.

Build up the fire. It's cold. Build up the fire. We'll do what we can. Sabina, get some more wood. Come around the fire, everybody. At least the young ones may pull through. Henry, have you eaten something?

HENRY:

Yes, papa.

ANTROBUS:

Gladys, have you had some supper?

GLADYS:

I ate in the kitchen, papa.

ANTROBUS:

If you do come through this—what'll you be able to do? What do you know? Henry, did you take a good look at that wheel?

HENRY:

Yes, papa.

ANTROBUS:

Sitting down in his chair.

Six times two are—

HENRY:

—twelve; six times three are eighteen; six times four are—Papa, it's hot and cold. It makes my head all funny. It makes me sleepy.

ANTROBUS:

Gives him a cuff.

Wake up. I don't care if your head is sleepy. Six times four are twenty-four. Six times five are—

HENRY:

Thirty. Papa!

ANTROBUS:

Maggie, put something into Gladys' head on the chance she can use it.

MRS. ANTROBUS:

What do you mean, George?

ANTROBUS:

Six times six are thirty-six.

Teach her the beginning of the Bible.

GLADYS:

But, Mama, it's so cold and close.

HENRY *has all but drowsed off. His father slaps him sharply and the lesson goes on.*

MRS. ANTROBUS:

"In the beginning God created the heavens and the earth; and the earth was waste and void; and the darkness was upon the face of the deep—"

The singing starts up again louder. SABINA *has returned with wood.*

SABINA:

After placing wood on the fireplace comes down to the footlights and addresses the audience:

Will you please start handing up your chairs? We'll need everything for this fire. Save the human race.—Ushers, will you pass the chairs up here? Thank you.

HENRY:

Six times nine are fifty-four; six times ten are sixty.

In the back of the auditorium the sound of chairs being ripped up can be heard. USHERS *rush down the aisles with chairs and hand them over.*

GLADYS:

"And God called the light Day and the darkness he called Night."

SABINA:

Pass up your chairs, everybody. Save the human race.

CURTAIN

—⚭—

Act II

Toward the end of the intermission, though with the houselights still up, lantern slide projections begin to appear on the curtain. Timetables for trains leaving Pennsylvania Station for Atlantic City. Advertisements of Atlantic City hotels, drugstores, churches, rug merchants; fortune tellers, Bingo parlors.

When the houselights go down, the voice of an ANNOUNCER *is heard.*

ANNOUNCER:

The Management now brings you the News Events of the World. Atlantic City, New Jersey:

Projection of a chrome postcard of the waterfront, trimmed in mica with the legend: FUN AT THE BEACH.

This great convention city is playing host this week to the anniversary convocation of that great fraternal order,—the Ancient and Honorable Order of Mammals, Subdivision Humans. This great fraternal, militant and burial society is celebrating on the Boardwalk, ladies and gentlemen, its six hundred thousandth Annual Convention.

It has just elected its president for the ensuing term,—

Projection of MR. *and* MRS. ANTROBUS *posed as they will be shown a few moments later.*

Mr. George Antrobus of Excelsior, New Jersey. We show you President Antrobus and his gracious and charming wife, every inch a mammal. Mr. Antrobus has had a long and chequered career. Credit has been paid to him for many useful enterprises including the introduction of the lever, of the wheel and the brewing of beer. Credit has been also extended to President Antrobus's gracious and charming wife for many practical suggestions, including the hem, the gore, and the gusset; and the novelty of the year,—frying in oil. Before we show you Mr. Antrobus accepting the nomination, we have an important announcement to make. As many of you know, this great celebration of the Order of the Mammals has received delegations from the other rival Orders,—or shall we say: esteemed concurrent Orders: the WINGS, the FINS, the SHELLS, and so on. These Orders are holding their conventions also, in various parts of the world, and have sent representatives to our own, two of a kind.

Later in the day we will show you President Antrobus broadcasting his words of greeting and congratulation to the collected assemblies of the whole natural world.

Ladies and Gentlemen! We give you President Antrobus!

The screen becomes a Transparency. MR. ANTROBUS *stands beside a pedestal;* MRS. ANTROBUS *is seated wearing a corsage of orchids.* ANTROBUS *wears an untidy Prince Albert; spats; from a red rosette in his buttonhole hangs a fine long purple ribbon of honor. He wears a gay lodge hat,—something between a fez and a legionnaire's cap.*

ANTROBUS:

Fellow-mammals, fellow-vertebrates, fellow-humans, I thank

you. Little did my dear parents think,—when they told me to stand on my own two feet,—that I'd arrive at this place.

My friends, we have come a long way.

During this week of happy celebration it is perhaps not fitting that we dwell on some of the difficult times we have been through. The dinosaur is extinct—

Applause.

—the ice has retreated; and the common cold is being pursued by every means within our power.

MRS. ANTROBUS *sneezes, laughs prettily, and murmurs: "I beg your pardon."*

In our memorial service yesterday we did honor to all our friends and relatives who are no longer with us, by reason of cold, earthquakes, plagues and . . . and . . .

Coughs.

differences of opinion.

As our Bishop so ably said . . . uh . . . so ably said. . . .

MRS. ANTROBUS:
Closed lips.

Gone, but not forgotten.

ANTROBUS:
'They are gone, but not forgotten.'

I think I can say, I think I can prophesy with complete . . . uh . . . with complete. . . .

MRS. ANTROBUS:
Confidence.

ANTROBUS:

Thank you, my dear,—With complete lack of confidence, that a new day of security is about to dawn.

The watchword of the closing year was: Work. I give you the watchword for the future: Enjoy Yourselves.

MRS. ANTROBUS:

George, sit down!

ANTROBUS:

Before I close, however, I wish to answer one of those unjust and malicious accusations that were brought against me during this last electoral campaign.

Ladies and gentlemen, the charge was made that at various points in my career I leaned toward joining some of the rival orders,—that's a lie.

As I told reporters of the *Atlantic City Herald,* I do not deny that a few months before my birth I hesitated between . . . uh . . . between pinfeathers and gill-breathing,—and so did many of us here,—but for the last million years I have been viviparous, hairy and diaphragmatic.

Applause. Cries of "Good old Antrobus," "The Prince chap!" "Georgie," etc.

ANNOUNCER:

Thank you. Thank you very much, Mr. Antrobus.

Now I know that our visitors will wish to hear a word from that gracious and charming mammal, Mrs. Antrobus, wife and mother,—Mrs. Antrobus!

MRS. ANTROBUS *rises, lays her program on her chair, bows and says:*

MRS. ANTROBUS:

Dear friends, I don't really think I should say anything. After all, it was my husband who was elected and not I. Perhaps, as president of the Women's Auxiliary Bed and Board Society,—I had some notes here, oh, yes, here they are:—I should give a short report from some of our committees that have been meeting in this beautiful city.

Perhaps it may interest you to know that it has at last been decided that the tomato is edible. Can you all hear me? The tomato *is* edible.

A delegate from across the sea reports that the thread woven by the silkworm gives a cloth . . . I have a sample of it here . . . can you see it? smooth, elastic. I should say that it's rather attractive,—though personally I prefer less shiny surfaces. Should the windows of a sleeping apartment be open or shut? I know all mothers will follow our debates on this matter with close interest. I am sorry to say that the most expert authorities have not yet decided. It does seem to me that the night air would be bound to be unhealthy for our children, but there are many distinguished authorities on both sides. Well, I could go on talking forever,—as Shakespeare says: a woman's work is seldom done; but I think I'd better join my husband in saying thank you, and sit down. Thank you.

She sits down.

ANNOUNCER:
Oh, Mrs. Antrobus!

MRS. ANTROBUS:
Yes?

ANNOUNCER:
We understand that you are about to celebrate a wedding anniversary. I know our listeners would like to extend their felicitations and hear a few words from you on that subject.

MRS. ANTROBUS:

I have been asked by this kind gentleman . . . yes, my friends, this Spring Mr. Antrobus and I will be celebrating our five thousandth wedding anniversary.

I don't know if I speak for my husband, but I can say that, as for me, I regret every moment of it.

Laughter of confusion.

I beg your pardon. What I *mean* to say is that I do not regret one moment of it. I hope none of you catch my cold. We have two children. We've always had two children, though it hasn't always been the same two. But as I say, we have two fine children, and we're very grateful for that. Yes, Mr. Antrobus and I have been married five thousand years. Each wedding anniversary reminds me of the times when there were no weddings. We had to crusade for marriage. Perhaps there are some women within the sound of my voice who remember that crusade and those struggles; we fought for it, didn't we? We chained ourselves to lampposts and we made disturbances in the Senate,— anyway, at last we women got the ring.

A few men helped us, but I must say that most men blocked our way at every step: they said we were unfeminine.

I only bring up these unpleasant memories, because I see some signs of backsliding from that great victory.

Oh, my fellow mammals, keep hold of that.

My husband says that the watchword for the year is Enjoy Yourselves. I think that's very open to misunderstanding. My watchword for the year is: Save the Family. It's held together for over five thousand years: Save it! Thank you.

ANNOUNCER:

Thank you, Mrs. Antrobus.

The transparency disappears.

We had hoped to show you the Beauty Contest that took place here today.

President Antrobus, an experienced judge of pretty girls, gave the title of Miss Atlantic City 1942, to Miss Lily-Sabina Fairweather, charming hostess of our Boardwalk Bingo Parlor.

Unfortunately, however, our time is up, and I must take you to some views of the Convention City and conveeners,—enjoying themselves.

A burst of music; the curtain rises.

The Boardwalk. The audience is sitting in the ocean. A handrail of scarlet cord stretches across the front of the stage. A ramp— also with scarlet handrail—descends to the right corner of the orchestra pit where a great scarlet beach umbrella or a cabana stands. Front and right stage left are benches facing the sea; attached to each bench is a street-lamp.

The only scenery is two cardboard cut-outs six feet high, representing shops at the back of the stage. Reading from left to right they are: SALT WATER TAFFY; FORTUNE TELLER; then the blank space; BINGO PARLOR; TURKISH BATH. They have practical doors, that of the Fortune Teller's being hung with bright gypsy curtains.

By the left proscenium and rising from the orchestra pit is the weather signal; it is like the mast of a ship with cross bars. From time to time black discs are hung on it to indicate the storm and hurricane warnings. Three roller chairs, pushed by melancholy NEGROES *file by empty. Throughout the act they traverse the stage in both directions.*

From time to time, CONVEENERS, *dressed like* MR. ANTROBUS, *cross the stage. Some walk sedately by; others engage in inane horseplay. The old gypsy* FORTUNE TELLER *is seated at the door of her shop, smoking a corncob pipe.*

From the Bingo Parlor comes the voice of the CALLER.

BINGO CALLER:

A-Nine; A-Nine. C-Twenty-six; C-Twenty-six.

A-Four; A-Four. B-Twelve.

CHORUS:
Back-stage.

Bingo!!!

The front of the Bingo Parlor shudders, rises a few feet in the air and returns to the ground trembling.

FORTUNE TELLER:
Mechanically, to the unconscious back of a passerby, pointing with her pipe.

Bright's disease! Your partner's deceiving you in that Kansas City deal. You'll have six grandchildren. Avoid high places.

She rises and shouts after another:

Cirrhosis of the liver!

SABINA *appears at the door of the Bingo Parlor. She hugs about her a blue raincoat that almost conceals her red bathing suit. She tries to catch the* FORTUNE TELLER'S *attention.*

SABINA:
Ssssst! Esmeralda! Ssssst!

FORTUNE TELLER:
Keck!

SABINA:
Has President Antrobus come along yet?

FORTUNE TELLER:

No, no, no. Get back there. Hide yourself.

SABINA:

I'm afraid I'll miss him. Oh, Esmeralda, if I fail in this, I'll die; I know I'll die. President Antrobus!!! And I'll be his wife! If it's the last thing I'll do, I'll be Mrs. George Antrobus.—Esmeralda, tell me my future.

FORTUNE TELLER:

Keck!

SABINA:

All right, I'll tell *you* my future.

Laughing dreamily and tracing it out with one finger on the palm of her hand.

I've won the Beauty Contest in Atlantic City,—well, I'll win the Beauty Contest of the whole world. I'll take President Antrobus away from that wife of his. Then I'll take every man away from his wife. I'll turn the whole earth upside down.

FORTUNE TELLER:

Keck!

SABINA:

When all those husbands just think about me they'll get dizzy. They'll faint in the streets. They'll have to lean against lamp-posts.—Esmeralda, who was Helen of Troy?

FORTUNE TELLER:

Furiously.

Shut your foolish mouth. When Mr. Antrobus comes along you can see what you can do. Until then,—go away.

SABINA *laughs. As she returns to the door of her Bingo Parlor a group of* CONVEENERS *rush over and smother her with atten-*

tions: "Oh, Miss Lily, you know me. You've known me for years."

SABINA:

Go away, boys, go away. I'm after bigger fry than you are.—Why, Mr. Simpson!! How *dare* you!! I expect that even you nobodies must have girls to amuse you; but where you find them and what you do with them, is of absolutely no interest to me.

Exit. The CONVEENERS *squeal with pleasure and stumble in after her.*

The FORTUNE TELLER *rises, puts her pipe down on the stool, unfurls her voluminous skirts, gives a sharp wrench to her bodice and strolls toward the audience, swinging her hips like a young woman.*

FORTUNE TELLER:

I tell the future. Keck. Nothing easier. Everybody's future is in their face. Nothing easier.

But who can tell your past,—eh? Nobody!

Your youth,—where did it go? It slipped away while you weren't looking. While you were asleep. While you were drunk? Puh! You're like our friends, Mr. and Mrs. Antrobus; you lie awake nights trying to know your past. What did it mean? What was it trying to say to you?

Think! Think! Split your heads. I can't tell the past and neither can you. If anybody tries to tell you the past, take my word for it, they're charlatans! Charlatans! But I can tell the future.

She suddenly barks at a passing chair-pusher.

Apoplexy!

She returns to the audience.

Nobody listens.—Keck! I see a face among you now—I won't embarrass him by pointing him out, but, listen, it may be you: Next year the watchsprings inside you will crumple up. Death by regret,—Type Y. It's in the corners of your mouth. You'll decide that you should have lived for pleasure, but that you missed it. Death by regret,—Type Y. . . . Avoid mirrors. You'll try to be angry,—but no!—no anger.

Far forward, confidentially.

And now what's the immediate future of our friends, the Antrobuses? Oh, you've seen it as well as I have, keck,—that dizziness of the head; that Great Man dizziness? The inventor of beer and gunpowder. The sudden fits of temper and then the long stretches of inertia? "I'm a sultan; let my slavegirls fan me?"

You know as well as I what's coming. Rain. Rain. Rain in floods. The deluge. But first you'll see shameful things—shameful things. Some of you will be saying: "Let him drown. He's not worth saving. Give the whole thing up." I can see it in your faces. But you're wrong. Keep your doubts and despairs to yourselves.

Again there'll be the narrow escape. The survival of a handful. From destruction,—total destruction.

She points sweeping with her hand to the stage.

Even of the animals, a few will be saved: two of a kind, male and female, two of a kind.

The heads of CONVEENERS *appear about the stage and in the orchestra pit, jeering at her.*

CONVEENERS:
Charlatan! Madam Kill-joy! Mrs. Jeremiah! Charlatan!

FORTUNE TELLER:
And *you!* Mark my words before it's too late. Where'll *you* be?

CONVEENERS:

The croaking raven. Old dust and ashes. Rags, bottles, sacks.

FORTUNE TELLER:

Yes, stick out your tongues. You can't stick your tongues out far enough to lick the death-sweat from your foreheads. It's too late to work now—bail out the flood with your soup spoons. You've had your chance and you've lost.

CONVEENERS:

Enjoy yourselves!!!

They disappear. The FORTUNE TELLER *looks off left and puts her finger on her lip.*

FORTUNE TELLER:

They're coming—the Antrobuses. Keck. Your hope. Your despair. Your selves.

Enter from the left, MR. *and* MRS. ANTROBUS *and* GLADYS.

MRS. ANTROBUS:

Gladys Antrobus, stick your stummick in.

GLADYS:

But it's easier this way.

MRS. ANTROBUS:

Well, it's too bad the new president has such a clumsy daughter, that's all I can say. Try and be a lady.

FORTUNE TELLER:

Aijah! That's been said a hundred billion times.

MRS. ANTROBUS:

Goodness! Where's Henry? He was here just a minute ago. Henry!

Sudden violent stir. A roller-chair appears from the left. About it are dancing in great excitement HENRY *and a* NEGRO CHAIR-PUSHER.

HENRY:
Slingshot in hand.

I'll put your eye out. I'll make you yell, like you never yelled before.

NEGRO:
At the same time.

Now, I warns you. I warns you. If you make me mad, you'll get hurt.

ANTROBUS:
Henry! What is this? Put down that slingshot.

MRS. ANTROBUS:
At the same time.

Henry! HENRY! Behave yourself.

FORTUNE TELLER:
That's right, young man. There are too many people in the world as it is. Everybody's in the way, except one's self.

HENRY:
All I wanted to do was—have some fun.

NEGRO:
Nobody can't touch my chair, nobody, without I allow 'em to. You get clean away from me and you get away fast.

He pushes his chair off, muttering.

ANTROBUS:
What were you doing, Henry?

HENRY:

Everybody's always getting mad. Everybody's always trying to push you around. I'll make him sorry for this; I'll make him sorry.

ANTROBUS:

Give me that slingshot.

HENRY:

I won't. I'm sorry I came to this place. I wish I weren't here. I wish I weren't anywhere.

MRS. ANTROBUS:

Now, Henry, don't get so excited about nothing. I declare I don't know what we're going to do with you. Put your slingshot in your pocket, and don't try to take hold of things that don't belong to you.

ANTROBUS:

After this you can stay home. I wash my hands of you.

MRS. ANTROBUS:

Come now, let's forget all about it. Everybody take a good breath of that sea air and calm down.

A passing CONVEENER *bows to* ANTROBUS *who nods to him.*

Who was that you spoke to, George?

ANTROBUS:

Nobody, Maggie. Just the candidate who ran against me in the election.

MRS. ANTROBUS:

The man who ran against you in the election!!

She turns and waves her umbrella after the disappearing CON-VEENER.

My husband didn't speak to you and he never will speak to you.

ANTROBUS:

Now, Maggie.

MRS. ANTROBUS:

After those lies you told about him in your speeches! Lies, that's what they were.

GLADYS AND HENRY:

Mama, everybody's looking at you. Everybody's laughing at you.

MRS. ANTROBUS:

If you must know, my husband's a SAINT, a downright SAINT, and you're not fit to speak to him on the street.

ANTROBUS:

Now, Maggie, now, Maggie, that's enough of that.

MRS. ANTROBUS:

George Antrobus, you're a perfect worm. If you won't stand up for yourself, I will.

GLADYS:

Mama, you just act awful in public.

MRS. ANTROBUS:
Laughing.

Well, I must say I enjoyed it. I feel better. Wish his wife had been there to hear it. Children, what do you want to do?

GLADYS:

Papa, can we ride in one of those chairs? Mama, I want to ride in one of those chairs.

MRS. ANTROBUS:

No, sir. If you're tired you just sit where you are. We have no money to spend on foolishness.

ANTROBUS:

I guess we have money enough for a thing like that. It's one of the things you do at Atlantic City.

MRS. ANTROBUS:

Oh, we have? I tell you it's a miracle my children have shoes to stand up in. I didn't think I'd ever live to see them pushed around in chairs.

ANTROBUS:

We're on a vacation, aren't we? We have a right to some treats, I guess. Maggie, someday you're going to drive me crazy.

MRS. ANTROBUS:

All right, go. I'll just sit here and laugh at you. And you can give me my dollar right in my hand. Mark my words, a rainy day is coming. There's a rainy day ahead of us. I feel it in my bones. Go on, throw your money around. I can starve. I've starved before. I know how.

A CONVEENER *puts his head through Turkish Bath window, and says with raised eyebrows:*

CONVEENER:

Hello, George. How are ya? I see where you brought the WHOLE family along.

MRS. ANTROBUS:

And what do you mean by that?

CONVEENER *withdraws head and closes window.*

ANTROBUS:

Maggie, I tell you there's a limit to what I can stand. God's Heaven, haven't I worked *enough*? Don't I get *any* vacation? Can't I even give my children so much as a ride in a roller-chair?

MRS. ANTROBUS:

Putting out her hand for raindrops.

Anyway, it's going to rain very soon and you have your broadcast to make.

ANTROBUS:

Now, Maggie, I warn you. A man can stand a family only just so long. I'm warning you.

Enter SABINA *from the Bingo Parlor. She wears a flounced red silk bathing suit, 1905. Red stockings, shoes, parasol. She bows demurely to* ANTROBUS *and starts down the ramp.* ANTROBUS *and the* CHILDREN *stare at her.* ANTROBUS *bows gallantly.*

MRS. ANTROBUS:

Why, George Antrobus, how can you say such a thing! You have the best family in the world.

ANTROBUS:

Good morning, Miss Fairweather.

SABINA *finally disappears behind the beach umbrella or in a cabana in the orchestra pit.*

MRS. ANTROBUS:

Who on earth was that you spoke to, George?

ANTROBUS:

Complacent; mock-modest.

Hm . . . m . . . just a . . . solambaka keray.

MRS. ANTROBUS:

What? I can't understand you.

GLADYS:

Mama, wasn't she beautiful?

HENRY:

Papa, introduce her to me.

MRS. ANTROBUS:

Children, will you be quiet while I ask your father a simple question?—Who did you say it was, George?

ANTROBUS:

Why-uh . . . a friend of mine. Very nice refined girl.

MRS. ANTROBUS:

I'm waiting.

ANTROBUS:

Maggie, that's the girl I gave the prize to in the beauty contest,—that's Miss Atlantic City 1942.

MRS. ANTROBUS:

Hm! She looked like Sabina to me.

HENRY:

At the railing.

Mama, the life-guard knows her, too. Mama, he knows her well.

ANTROBUS:

Henry, come here.—She's a very nice girl in every way and the sole support of her aged mother.

MRS. ANTROBUS:

So was Sabina, so was Sabina; and it took a wall of ice to open your eyes about Sabina.—Henry, come over and sit down on this bench.

ANTROBUS:

She's a very different matter from Sabina. Miss Fairweather is a college graduate, Phi Beta Kappa.

MRS. ANTROBUS:

Henry, you sit here by mama. Gladys—

ANTROBUS:

Sitting.

Reduced circumstances have required her taking a position as hostess in a Bingo Parlor; but there isn't a girl with higher principles in the country.

MRS. ANTROBUS:

Well, let's not talk about it.—Henry, I haven't seen a whale yet.

ANTROBUS:

She speaks seven languages and has more culture in her little finger than you've acquired in a lifetime.

MRS. ANTROBUS:

Assumed amiability.

All right, all right, George. I'm glad to know there are such superior girls in the Bingo Parlors.—Henry, what's that?

Pointing at the storm signal, which has one black disk.

HENRY:

What is it, Papa?

ANTROBUS:

What? Oh, that's the storm signal. One of those black disks means bad weather; two means storm; three means hurricane; and four means the end of the world.

As they watch it a second black disk rolls into place.

MRS. ANTROBUS:

Goodness! I'm going this very minute to buy you all some raincoats.

GLADYS:

Putting her cheek against her father's shoulder.

Mama, don't go yet. I like sitting this way. And the ocean coming in and coming in. Papa, don't you like it?

MRS. ANTROBUS:

Well, there's only one thing I lack to make me a perfectly happy woman: I'd like to see a whale.

HENRY:

Mama, we saw two. Right out there. They're delegates to the convention. I'll find you one.

GLADYS:

Papa, ask me something. Ask me a question.

ANTROBUS:

Well . . . how big's the ocean?

GLADYS:

Papa, you're teasing me. It's—three-hundred and sixty million square-miles—and—it—covers—three-fourths—of—the—earth's—surface—and—its—deepest-place—is—five—and—a—half—miles—deep—and—its—average—depth—is—twelve—thousand—feet. No, Papa, ask me something hard, real hard.

MRS. ANTROBUS:

Rising.

Now I'm going off to buy those raincoats. I think that bad weather's going to get worse and worse. I hope it doesn't come before your broadcast. I should think we have about an hour or so.

HENRY:

I hope it comes and zzzzzz everything before it. I hope it—

MRS. ANTROBUS:

Henry!—George, I think . . . maybe, it's one of those storms that are just as bad on land·as on the sea. When you're just as safe and safer in a good stout boat.

HENRY:

There's a boat out at the end of the pier.

MRS. ANTROBUS:

Well, keep your eye on it. George, you shut your eyes and get a good rest before the broadcast.

ANTROBUS:

Thundering Judas, do I have to be told when to open and shut my eyes? Go and buy your raincoats.

MRS. ANTROBUS:

Now, children, you have ten minutes to walk around. Ten minutes. And, Henry: control yourself. Gladys, stick by your brother and don't get lost.

They run off.

MRS. ANTROBUS:

Will you be all right, George?

CONVEENERS *suddenly stick their heads out of the Bingo Parlor and Salt Water Taffy store, and voices rise from the orchestra pit.*

CONVEENERS:

George. Geo-r-r-rge! George! Leave the old hen-coop at home, George. Do-mes-ticated Georgie!

MRS. ANTROBUS:
Shaking her umbrella.

Low common oafs! That's what they are. Guess a man has a right to bring his wife to a convention, if he wants to.

She starts off.

What's the matter with a family, I'd like to know. What else have they got to offer?

Exit. ANTROBUS *has closed his eyes. The* FORTUNE TELLER *comes out of her shop and goes over to the left proscenium. She leans against it watching* SABINA *quizzically.*

FORTUNE TELLER:

Heh! Here she comes!

SABINA:

Loud whisper.

What's he doing?

FORTUNE TELLER:

Oh, he's ready for you. Bite your lips, dear, take a long breath and come on up.

SABINA:

I'm nervous. My whole future depends on this. I'm nervous.

FORTUNE TELLER:

Don't be a fool. What more could you want? He's forty-five. His head's a little dizzy. He's just been elected president. He's never known any other woman than his wife. Whenever he looks at her he realizes that she knows every foolish thing he's ever done.

SABINA:

Still whispering.

I don't know why it is, but every time I start one of these I'm nervous.

The FORTUNE TELLER *stands in the center of the stage watching the following:*

FORTUNE TELLER:

You make me tired.

SABINA:

First tell me my fortune.

The FORTUNE TELLER *laughs drily and makes the gesture of brushing away a nonsensical question.* SABINA *coughs and says:*

Oh, Mr. Antrobus,—dare I speak to you for a moment?

ANTROBUS:

What?—Oh, certainly, certainly, Miss Fairweather.

SABINA:

Mr. Antrobus . . . I've been so unhappy. I've wanted . . . I've wanted to make sure that you don't think that I'm the kind of girl who goes out for beauty contests.

FORTUNE TELLER:

That's the way!

ANTROBUS:

Oh, I understand. I understand perfectly.

FORTUNE TELLER:

Give it a little more. Lean on it.

SABINA:

I knew you would. My mother said to me this morning: Lily, she said, that fine Mr. Antrobus gave you the prize because he saw at once that you weren't the kind of girl who'd go in for a thing like that. But, honestly, Mr. Antrobus, in this world, honestly, a good girl doesn't know where to turn.

FORTUNE TELLER:

Now you've gone too far.

ANTROBUS:

My dear Miss Fairweather!

SABINA:

You wouldn't know how hard it is. With that lovely wife and daughter you have. Oh, I think Mrs. Antrobus is the finest woman I ever saw. I wish I were like her.

ANTROBUS:

There, there. There's . . . uh . . . room for all kinds of people in the world, Miss Fairweather.

SABINA:

How wonderful of you to say that. How generous!—Mr. Antrobus, have you a moment free? . . . I'm afraid I may be a little conspicuous here . . . could you come down, for just a moment, to my beach cabana . . . ?

ANTROBUS:

Why-uh . . . yes, certainly . . . for a moment . . . just for a moment.

SABINA:

There's a deck chair there. Because: you know you *do* look tired. Just this morning my mother said to me: Lily, she said, I hope Mr. Antrobus is getting a good rest. His fine strong face has deep deep lines in it. Now isn't it true, Mr. Antrobus: you work too hard?

FORTUNE TELLER:

Bingo!

She goes into her shop.

SABINA:

Now you will just stretch out. No, I shan't say a word, not a word. I shall just sit there,—privileged. That's what I am.

ANTROBUS:
Taking her hand.

Miss Fairweather . . . you'll . . . spoil me.

SABINA:

Just a moment. I have something I wish to say to the audience.—Ladies and gentlemen. I'm not going to play this particular scene tonight. It's just a short scene and we're going to skip it. But I'll tell you what takes place and then we can continue the play from there on. Now in this scene—

ANTROBUS:

Between his teeth.

But, Miss Somerset!

SABINA:

I'm sorry. I'm sorry. But I have to skip it. In this scene, I talk to Mr. Antrobus, and at the end of it he decides to leave his wife, get a divorce at Reno and marry me. That's all.

ANTROBUS:

Fitz!—Fitz!

SABINA:

So that now I've told you we can jump to the end of it,—where you say:

Enter in fury MR. FITZPATRICK, *the stage manager.*

MR. FITZPATRICK:

Miss Somerset, we insist on your playing this scene.

SABINA:

I'm sorry, Mr. Fitzpatrick, but I can't and I won't. I've told the audience all they need to know and now we can go on.

Other ACTORS *begin to appear on the stage, listening.*

MR. FITZPATRICK:

And *why* can't you play it?

SABINA:

Because there are some lines in that scene that would hurt some people's feelings and I don't think the theatre is a place where people's feelings ought to be hurt.

MR. FITZPATRICK:

Miss Somerset, you can pack up your things and go home. I shall call the understudy and I shall report you to Equity.

SABINA:

I sent the understudy up to the corner for a cup of coffee and if Equity tries to penalize me I'll drag the case right up to the Supreme Court. Now listen, everybody, there's no need to get excited.

MR. FITZPATRICK AND ANTROBUS:

Why can't you play it . . . what's the matter with the scene?

SABINA:

Well, if you must know, I have a personal guest in the audience tonight. Her life hasn't been exactly a happy one. I wouldn't have my friend hear some of these lines for the whole world. I don't suppose it occurred to the author that some other women might have gone through the experience of losing their husbands like this. Wild horses wouldn't drag from me the details of my friend's life, but . . . well, they'd been married twenty years, and before he got rich, why, she'd done the washing and everything.

MR. FITZPATRICK:

Miss Somerset, your friend will forgive you. We must play this scene.

SABINA:

Nothing, nothing will make me say some of those lines . . . about "a man outgrows a wife every seven years" and . . . and that one about "the Mohammedans being the only people who looked the subject square in the face." Nothing.

MR. FITZPATRICK:

Miss Somerset! Go to your dressing room. I'll *read* your lines.

SABINA:

Now everybody's nerves are on edge.

MR. ANTROBUS:

Skip the scene.

MR. FITZPATRICK *and the other* ACTORS *go off.*

SABINA:

Thank you. I knew you'd understand. We'll do just what I said. So Mr. Antrobus is going to divorce his wife and marry me. Mr. Antrobus, you say: "It won't be easy to lay all this before my wife."

The ACTORS *withdraw.* ANTROBUS *walks about, his hand to his forehead muttering:*

ANTROBUS:

Wait a minute. I can't get back into it as easily as all that. "My wife is a very obstinate woman." Hm . . . then you say . . . hm . . . Miss Fairweather, I mean Lily, it won't be easy to lay all this before my wife. It'll hurt her feelings a little.

SABINA:

Listen, George: *other* people haven't got feelings. Not in the same way that we have,—we who are presidents like you and prize-winners like me. Listen, other people haven't got feelings; they just imagine they have. Within two weeks they go back to playing bridge and going to the movies.

Listen, dear: everybody in the world except a few people like you and me are just people of straw. Most people have no insides at all. Now that you're president you'll see that. Listen, darling, there's a kind of secret society at the top of the world,—like you and me,—that know this. The world was made for us. What's life anyway? Except for two things, pleasure and power, what is life? Boredom! Foolishness. You know it is. Except for those two things, life's nau-se-at-ing. So,—come here!

She moves close. They kiss.

So.

Now when your wife comes, it's really very simple; just tell her.

ANTROBUS:

Lily, Lily: you're a wonderful woman.

SABINA:

Of course I am.

They enter the cabana and it hides them from view. Distant roll of thunder. A third black disk appears on the weather signal. Distant thunder is heard. MRS. ANTROBUS *appears carrying parcels. She looks about, seats herself on the bench left, and fans herself with her handkerchief. Enter* GLADYS *right, followed by two* CONVEENERS. *She is wearing red stockings.*

MRS. ANTROBUS:

Gladys!

GLADYS:

Mama, here I am.

MRS. ANTROBUS:

Gladys Antrobus!!! Where did you get those dreadful things?

GLADYS:

Wha-a-t? Papa liked the color.

MRS. ANTROBUS:

You go back to the hotel this minute!

GLADYS:

I won't. I won't. Papa liked the color.

MRS. ANTROBUS:

All right. All right. You stay here. I've a good mind to let your father see you that way. You stay right here.

GLADYS:

I . . . I don't want to stay if . . . if you don't think he'd like it.

MRS. ANTROBUS:

Oh . . . it's all one to me. I don't care what happens. I don't care if the biggest storm in the whole world comes. Let it come.

She folds her hands.

Where's your brother?

GLADYS:

In a small voice.

He'll be here.

MRS. ANTROBUS:

Will he? Well, let him get into trouble. I don't care. I don't know where your father is, I'm sure.

Laughter from the cabana.

GLADYS:

Leaning over the rail.

I think he's . . . Mama, he's talking to the lady in the red dress.

MRS. ANTROBUS:

Is that so?

Pause.

We'll wait till he's through. Sit down here beside me and stop fidgeting . . . what are you crying about?

Distant thunder. She covers GLADYS' *stockings with a raincoat.*

GLADYS:

You don't like my stockings.

Two CONVEENERS *rush in with a microphone on a standard and various paraphernalia. The* FORTUNE TELLER *appears at the door of her shop. Other characters gradually gather.*

BROADCAST OFFICIAL:

Mrs. Antrobus! Thank God we've found you at last. Where's Mr. Antrobus? We've been hunting everywhere for him. It's about time for the broadcast to the conventions of the world.

MRS. ANTROBUS:

Calm.

I expect he'll be here in a minute.

BROADCAST OFFICIAL:

Mrs. Antrobus, if he doesn't show up in time, I hope you will consent to broadcast in his place. It's the most important broadcast of the year.

SABINA *enters from cabana followed by* ANTROBUS.

MRS. ANTROBUS:

No, I shan't. I haven't one single thing to say.

BROADCAST OFFICIAL:

Then won't you help us find him, Mrs. Antrobus? A storm's coming up. A hurricane. A deluge!

SECOND CONVEENER:

Who has sighted ANTROBUS *over the rail.*

Joe! Joe! Here he is.

BROADCAST OFFICIAL:

In the name of God, Mr. Antrobus, you're on the air in five minutes. Will you kindly please come and test the instrument? That's all we ask. If you just please begin the alphabet slowly.

> ANTROBUS, *with set face, comes ponderously up the ramp. He stops at the point where his waist is level with the stage and speaks authoritatively to the* OFFICIALS.

ANTROBUS:

I'll be ready when the time comes. Until then, move away. Go away. I have something I wish to say to my wife.

BROADCASTING OFFICIAL:
Whimpering.

Mr. Antrobus! This is the most important broadcast of the year.

> *The* OFFICIALS *withdraw to the edge of the stage.* SABINA *glides up the ramp behind* ANTROBUS.

SABINA:
Whispering.

Don't let her argue. Remember arguments have nothing to do with it.

ANTROBUS:

Maggie, I'm moving out of the hotel. In fact, I'm moving out of everything. For good. I'm going to marry Miss Fair-weather. I shall provide generously for you and the children. In a few years you'll be able to see that it's all for the best. That's all I have to say.

BROADCAST OFFICAL:

Mr. Antrobus! I hope you'll be ready. This is the most important broadcast of the year.

BINGO ANNOUNCER:

A—nine; A—nine. D—forty-two; D—forty-two. C—thirty; C-thirty. B—seventeen; B—seventeen. C—forty; C-forty.

GLADYS:

What did Papa say, Mama? I didn't hear what papa said.

CHORUS:

Bingo!

BROADCAST OFFICIAL:

Mr. Antrobus. All we want to do is test your voice with the alphabet.

ANTROBUS:

Go away. Clear out.

MRS. ANTROBUS:

Composedly with lowered eyes.

George, I can't talk to you until you wipe those silly red marks off your face.

ANTROBUS:

I think there's nothing to talk about. I've said what I have to say.

SABINA:

Splendid!

ANTROBUS:

You're a fine woman, Maggie, but . . . but a man has his own life to lead in the world.

MRS. ANTROBUS:

Well, after living with you for five thousand years I guess I have a right to a word or two, haven't I?

ANTROBUS:

To SABINA.

What can I answer to that?

SABINA:

Tell her that conversation would only hurt her feelings. It's-kinder-in-the-long-run-to-do-it-short-and-quick.

ANTROBUS:

I want to spare your feelings in every way I can, Maggie.

BROADCAST OFFICIAL:

Mr. Antrobus, the hurricane signal's gone up. We could begin right now.

MRS. ANTROBUS:

Calmly, almost dreamily.

I didn't marry you because you were perfect. I didn't even marry you because I loved you. I married you because you gave me a promise.

She takes off her ring and looks at it.

That promise made up for your faults. And the promise I gave you made up for mine. Two imperfect people got married and it was the promise that made the marriage.

ANTROBUS:

Maggie, . . . I was only nineteen.

MRS. ANTROBUS:

She puts her ring back on her finger.

And when our children were growing up, it wasn't a house that protected them; and it wasn't our love, that protected them—it was that promise.

And when that promise is broken—this can happen!

With a sweep of the hand she removes the raincoat from GLADYS' *stockings.*

ANTROBUS:

Stretches out his arm, apoplectic.

Gladys!! Have you gone crazy? Has everyone gone crazy?

Turning on SABINA.

You did this. You gave them to her.

SABINA:

I never said a word to her.

ANTROBUS:

To GLADYS.

You go back to the hotel and take those horrible things off.

GLADYS:

Pert.

Before I go, I've got something to tell you,—it's about Henry.

MRS. ANTROBUS:

Claps her hands peremptorily.

Stop your noise,—I'm taking her back to the hotel, George. Before I go I have a letter. . . . I have a message to throw into the ocean.

Fumbling in her handbag.

Where is the plagued thing? Here it is.

She flings something—invisible to us—far over the heads of the audience to the back of the auditorium.

It's a bottle. And in the bottle's a letter. And in the letter is written all the things that a woman knows.

It's never been told to any man and it's never been told to any woman, and if it finds its destination, a new time will come. We're not what books and plays say we are. We're not what advertisements say we are. We're not in the movies and we're not on the radio.

We're not what you're all told and what you think we are:

We're ourselves. And if any man can find one of us he'll learn why the whole universe was set in motion. And if any man harm any one of us, his soul—the only soul he's got—had better be at the bottom of that ocean,—and that's the only way to put it. Gladys, come here. We're going back to the hotel.

> *She drags* GLADYS *firmly off by the hand, but* GLADYS *breaks away and comes down to speak to her father.*

SABINA:

Such goings-on. Don't give it a minute's thought.

GLADYS:

Anyway, I think you ought to know that Henry hit a man with a stone. He hit one of those colored men that push the chairs and the man's very sick. Henry ran away and hid and some police-men are looking for him very hard. And I don't care a bit if you don't want to have anything to do with mama and me, because I'll never like you again and I hope nobody ever likes you again,—so there!

> *She runs off.* ANTROBUS *starts after her.*

ANTROBUS:

I . . . I have to go and see what I can do about this.

SABINA:

You stay right here. Don't you go now while you're excited. Gracious sakes, all these things will be forgotten in a hundred years. Come, now, you're on the air. Just say anything,—it doesn't matter what. Just a lot of birds and fishes and things.

BROADCAST OFFICIAL:

Thank you, Miss Fairweather. Thank you very much. Ready, Mr. Antrobus.

ANTROBUS:
Touching the microphone.

What is it, what is it? Who am I talking to?

BROADCAST OFFICIAL:
Why, Mr. Antrobus! To our order and to all the other orders.

ANTROBUS:
Raising his head.

What are all those birds doing?

BROADCAST OFFICIAL:
Those are just a few of the birds. Those are the delegates to our convention,—two of a kind.

ANTROBUS:
Pointing into the audience.

Look at the water. Look at them all. Those fishes jumping. The children should see this!—There's Maggie's whales!! Here are your whales, Maggie!!

BROADCAST OFFICIAL:
I hope you're ready, Mr. Antrobus.

ANTROBUS:
And look on the beach! You didn't tell me these would be here!

SABINA:
Yes, George. Those are the animals.

BROADCAST OFFICIAL:
Busy with the apparatus.

Yes, Mr. Antrobus, those are the vertebrates. We hope the lion will have a word to say when you're through. Step right up, Mr. Antrobus, we're ready. We'll just have time before the storm.

Pause. In a hoarse whisper:

They're wait-ing.

It has grown dark. Soon after he speaks a high whistling noise begins. Strange veering lights start whirling about the stage. The other characters disappear from the stage.

ANTROBUS:

Friends. Cousins. Four score and ten billion years ago our fore-father brought forth upon this planet the spark of life,—

He is drowned out by thunder. When the thunder stops the FOR-TUNE TELLER *is seen standing beside him.*

FORTUNE TELLER:

Antrobus, there's not a minute to be lost. Don't you see the four disks on the weather signal? Take your family into that boat at the end of the pier.

ANTROBUS:

My family? I have no family. Maggie! Maggie! They won't come.

FORTUNE TELLER:

They'll come.—Antrobus! Take these animals into that boat with you. All of them,—two of each kind.

SABINA:

George, what's the matter with you? This is just a storm like any other storm.

ANTROBUS:

Maggie!

SABINA:

Stay with me, we'll go . . .

Losing conviction.

This is just another thunderstorm,—isn't it? Isn't it?

ANTROBUS:

Maggie!!!

MRS. ANTROBUS *appears beside him with* GLADYS.

MRS. ANTROBUS:
Matter-of-fact.

Here I am and here's Gladys.

ANTROBUS:

Where've you been? Where have you been? Quick, we're going into that boat out there.

MRS. ANTROBUS:

I know we are. But I haven't found Henry.

She wanders off into the darkness calling "Henry!"

SABINA:
Low urgent babbling, only occasionally raising her voice.

I don't believe it. I don't believe it's anything at all. I've seen hundreds of storms like this.

FORTUNE TELLER:

There's no time to lose. Go. Push the animals along before you. Start a new world. Begin again.

SABINA:

Esmeralda! George! Tell me,—is it really serious?

ANTROBUS:
Suddenly very busy.

Elephants first. Gently, gently.—Look where you're going.

GLADYS:
Leaning over the ramp and striking an animal on the back.

Stop it or you'll be left behind!

ANTROBUS:

Is the Kangaroo there? *There* you are! Take those turtles in your pouch, will you?

To some other animals, pointing to his shoulder.

Here! You jump up here. You'll be trampled on.

GLADYS:
To her father, pointing below.

Papa, look,—the snakes!

MRS. ANTROBUS:
I can't find Henry. Hen-ry!

ANTROBUS:

Go along. Go along. Climb on their backs.—Wolves! Jackals,— whatever you are,—tend to your own business!

GLADYS:
Pointing, tenderly.

Papa,—look.

SABINA:

Mr. Antrobus—take me with you. Don't leave me here. I'll work. I'll help. I'll do anything.

THREE CONVEENERS *cross the stage, marching with a banner.*

CONVEENERS:

George! What are you scared of?—George! Fellas, it looks like rain.—"Maggie, where's my umbrella?"—George, setting up for Barnum and Bailey.

ANTROBUS:

Again catching his wife's hand.

Come on now, Maggie,—the pier's going to break any minute.

MRS. ANTROBUS:

I'm not going a step without Henry. Henry!

GLADYS:

On the ramp.

Mama! Papa! Hurry. The pier's cracking, Mama. It's going to break.

MRS. ANTROBUS:

Henry! Cain! CAIN!

HENRY *dashes into the stage and joins his mother.*

HENRY:

Here I am, Mama.

MRS. ANTROBUS:

Thank God!—now come quick.

HENRY:

I didn't think you wanted me.

MRS. ANTROBUS:

Quick!

She pushes him down before her into the aisle.

SABINA:

All the ANTROBUSES *are now in the theater aisle.* SABINA *stands at the top of the ramp.*

Mrs. Antrobus, take me. Don't you remember me? I'll work. I'll help. Don't leave me here!

MRS. ANTROBUS:
Impatiently, but as though it were of no importance.

Yes, yes. There's a lot of work to be done. Only hurry.

FORTUNE TELLER:
Now dominating the stage. To SABINA *with a grim smile.*

Yes, go—back to the kitchen with you.

SABINA:
Half-down the ramp. To FORTUNE TELLER.

I don't know why my life's always being interrupted—just when everything's going fine!!

She dashes up the aisle.

Now the CONVENEERS *emerge doing a serpentine dance on the stage. They jeer at the* FORTUNE TELLER.

CONVEENERS:
Get a canoe—there's not a minute to be lost! Tell me my future, Mrs. Croaker.

FORTUNE TELLER:
Paddle in the water, boys—enjoy yourselves.

VOICE FROM THE BINGO PARLOR:
A-nine; A-nine. C-Twenty-four. C-Twenty-four.

CONVEENERS:
Rags, bottles, and sacks.

FORTUNE TELLER:
Go back and climb on your roofs. Put rags in the cracks under your doors.—Nothing will keep out the flood. You've had your chance. You've had your day. You've failed. You've lost.

VOICE FROM THE BINGO PARLOR:

B-fifteen. B-Fifteen.

FORTUNE TELLER:

Shading her eyes and looking out to sea.

They're safe. George Antrobus! Think it over! A new world to make—think it over!

CURTAIN

Act III

Just before the curtain rises, two sounds are heard from the stage: a cracked bugle call.

The curtain rises on almost total darkness. Almost all the flats composing the walls of MR. ANTROBUS' *house, as of Act I, are up, but they lean helter-skelter against one another, leaving irregular gaps. Among the flats missing are two in the back wall, leaving the frames of the window and door crazily out of line. Off stage, back right, some red Roman fire is burning. The bugle call is repeated. Enter* SABINA *through the tilted door. She is dressed as a Napoleonic camp follower, "la fille du regiment," in begrimed reds and blues.*

SABINA:

Mrs. Antrobus! Gladys! Where are you?

The war's over. The war's over. You can come out. The peace treaty's been signed.

Where are they?—Hmpf! Are they dead, too? Mrs. Annnntrobus! Glaaaadus! Mr. Antrobus'll be here this afternoon. I just saw him downtown. Huuuurry and put things in order. He says that now that the war's over we'll all have to settle down and be perfect.

Enter MR. FITZPATRICK, *the stage manager, followed by the whole company, who stand waiting at the edges of the stage.* MR. FITZ- PATRICK *tries to interrupt* SABINA.

MR. FITZPATRICK:

Miss Somerset, we have to stop a moment.

SABINA:

They may be hiding out in the back—

MR. FITZPATRICK:

Miss Somerset! We have to stop a moment.

SABINA:

What's the matter?

MR. FITZPATRICK:

There's an explanation we have to make to the audience.— Lights, please.

To the actor who plays MR. ANTROBUS,

Will you explain the matter to the audience?

The lights go up. We now see that a balcony or elevated runway has been erected at the back of the stage, back of the wall of the Antrobus house. From its extreme right and left ends ladder-like steps descend to the floor of the stage.

ANTROBUS:

Ladies and gentlemen, an unfortunate accident has taken place back stage. Perhaps I should say *another* unfortunate accident.

SABINA:

I'm sorry. I'm sorry.

ANTROBUS:

The management feels, in fact, we all feel that you are due an apology. And now we have to ask your indulgence for the most serious mishap of all. Seven of our actors have . . . have been taken ill. Apparently, it was something they ate. I'm not exactly clear what happened.

All the ACTORS *start to talk at once.* ANTROBUS *raises his hand.*

Now, now—not all at once. Fitz, do you know what it was?

MR. FITZPATRICK:

Why, it's perfectly clear. These seven actors had dinner together, and they ate something that disagreed with them.

SABINA:

Disagreed with them!!! They have ptomaine poisoning. They're in Bellevue Hospital this very minute in agony. They're having their stomachs pumped out this very minute, in perfect agony.

ANTROBUS:

Fortunately, we've just heard they'll all recover.

SABINA:

It'll be a miracle if they do, a downright miracle. It was the lemon meringue pie.

ACTORS:

It was the fish . . . it was the canned tomatoes . . . it was the fish.

SABINA:

It was the lemon meringue pie. I saw it with my own eyes; it had blue mould all over the bottom of it.

ANTROBUS:

Whatever it was, they're in no condition to take part in this performance. Naturally, we haven't enough understudies to fill all those roles; but we do have a number of splendid volunteers who have kindly consented to help us out. These friends have watched our rehearsals, and they assure me that they know the lines and the business very well. Let me introduce them to you— my dresser, Mr. Tremayne,—himself a distinguished Shakespearean actor for many years; our wardrobe mistress, Hester; Miss Somerset's maid, Ivy; and Fred Bailey, captain of the ushers in this theatre.

These persons bow modestly. IVY *and* HESTER *are colored girls.*

Now this scene takes place near the end of the act. And I'm sorry to say we'll need a short rehearsal, just a short run-through. And as some of it takes place in the auditorium, we'll have to keep the curtain up. Those of you who wish can go out in the lobby and smoke some more. The rest of you can listen to us, or . . . or just talk quietly among yourselves, as you choose. Thank you. Now will you take it over, Mr. Fitzpatrick?

MR. FITZPATRICK:

Thank you.—Now for those of you who are listening perhaps I should explain that at the end of this act, the men have come back from the War and the family's settled down in the house. And the author wants to show the hours of the night passing by over their heads, and the planets crossing the sky . . . uh . . . over their heads. And he says—this is hard to explain—that each of the hours of the night is a philosopher, or a great thinker. Eleven o'clock, for instance, is Aristotle. And nine o'clock is Spinoza. Like that. I don't suppose it means anything. It's just a kind of poetic effect.

SABINA:

Not mean anything! Why, it certainly does. Twelve o'clock goes by saying those wonderful things. I think it means that when people are asleep they have all those lovely thoughts, much better than when they're awake.

IVY:

Excuse me, I think it means,—excuse me, Mr. Fitzpatrick—

SABINA:

What were you going to say, Ivy?

IVY:

Mr. Fitzpatrick, you let my father come to a rehearsal; and my father's a Baptist minister, and he said that the author meant that—just like the hours and stars go by over our heads at night, in the same way the ideas and thoughts of the great men are in the air around us all the time and they're working on us, even when we don't know it.

MR. FITZPATRICK:

Well, well, maybe that's it. Thank you, Ivy. Anyway,—the hours of the night are philosophers. My friends, are you ready? Ivy, can you be eleven o'clock? "This good estate of the mind possessing its object in energy we call divine." Aristotle.

IVY:

Yes, sir. I know that and I know twelve o'clock and I know nine o'clock.

MR. FITZPATRICK:

Twelve o'clock? Mr. Tremayne, the Bible.

TREMAYNE:

Yes.

MR. FITZPATRICK:

Ten o'clock? Hester,—Plato?

She nods eagerly.

Nine o'clock, Spinoza,—Fred?

BAILEY:

Yes, *sir.*

FRED BAILEY *picks up a great gilded cardboard numeral IX and starts up the steps to the platform.* MR. FITZPATRICK *strikes his forehead.*

MR. FITZPATRICK:

The planets!! We forgot all about the planets.

SABINA:

O my God! The planets! Are they sick too?

ACTORS *nod.*

MR. FITZPATRICK:

Ladies and gentlemen, the planets are singers. Of course, we can't replace them, so you'll have to imagine them singing in this scene. Saturn sings from the orchestra pit down here. The Moon is way up there. And Mars with a red lantern in his hand, stands in the aisle over there—Tz-tz-tz. It's too bad; it all makes a very fine effect. However! Ready—nine o'clock: Spinoza.

BAILEY:

Walking slowly across the balcony, left to right.

"After experience had taught me that the common occurrences of daily life are vain and futile—"

FITZPATRICK:

Louder, Fred. "And I saw that all the objects of my desire and fear—"

BAILEY:

"And I saw that all the objects of my desire and fear were in themselves nothing good nor bad save insofar as the mind was affected by them—"

FITZPATRICK:

Do you know the rest? All right. Ten o'clock. Hester. Plato.

HESTER:

"Then tell me, O Critias, how will a man choose the ruler that shall rule over him? Will he not—"

FITZPATRICK:

Thank you. Skip to the end, Hester.

HESTER:

". . . can be multiplied a thousand fold in its effects among the citizens."

FITZPATRICK:

Thank you.—Aristotle, Ivy?

IVY:

"This good estate of the mind possessing its object in energy we call divine. This we mortals have occasionally and it is this energy which is pleasantest and best. But God has it always. It is wonderful in us; but in Him how much more wonderful."

FITZPATRICK:

Midnight. Midnight, Mr. Tremayne. That's right,—you've done it before.—All right, everybody. You know what you have to do.—Lower the curtain. Houselights up. Act Three of THE SKIN OF OUR TEETH.

As the curtain descends he is heard saying:

You volunteers, just wear what you have on. Don't try to put on the costumes today.

Houselights go down. The Act begins again. The Bugle call. Curtain rises. Enter SABINA.

SABINA:

Mrs. Antrobus! Gladys! Where are you? The war's over.—You've heard all this—

She gabbles the main points.

Where—are—they? Are—they—dead, too, et cetera. I—just—saw—Mr.—Antrobus—down town, et cetera.

Slowing up:

He says that now that the war's over we'll all have to settle down and be perfect. They may be hiding out in the back somewhere. Mrs. An-tro-bus.

She wanders off. It has grown lighter.

A trapdoor is cautiously raised and MRS. ANTROBUS *emerges waist-high and listens. She is disheveled and worn; she wears a tattered dress and a shawl half covers her head. She talks down through the trapdoor.*

MRS. ANTROBUS:

It's getting light. There's still something burning over there— Newark, or Jersey City. What? Yes, I could swear I heard someone moving about up here. But I can't see anybody. I say: I can't see anybody.

She starts to move about the stage. GLADYS' *head appears at the trapdoor. She is holding a* BABY.

GLADYS:

Oh, Mama. Be careful.

MRS. ANTROBUS:

Now, Gladys, you stay out of sight.

GLADYS:

Well, let me stay here just a minute. I want the baby to get some of this fresh air.

MRS. ANTROBUS:

All right, but keep your eyes open. I'll see what I can find. I'll have a good hot plate of soup for you before you can say Jack Robinson. Gladys Antrobus! Do you know what I think I see? There's old Mr. Hawkins sweeping the sidewalk in front of his A. and P. store. Sweeping it with a broom. Why, he must have gone crazy, like the others! I see some other people moving about, too.

GLADYS:

Mama, come back, come back.

MRS. ANTROBUS *returns to the trapdoor and listens.*

MRS. ANTROBUS:

Gladys, there's something in the air. Everybody's movement's sort of different. I see some women walking right out in the middle of the street.

SABINA'S VOICE:

Mrs. An-tro-bus!

MRS. ANTROBUS AND GLADYS:

What's that?!!

SABINA'S VOICE:

Glaaaadys! Mrs. An-tro-bus!

Enter SABINA.

MRS. ANTROBUS:

Gladys, that's Sabina's voice as sure as I live.—Sabina! Sabina!— Are you *alive*?!!

SABINA:

Of course, I'm alive. How've you girls been?—*Don't* try and kiss me. I never want to kiss another human being as long as I live. Sh-sh, there's nothing to get emotional about. Pull yourself together, the war's over. Take a deep breath,—the war's over.

MRS. ANTROBUS:

The war's over!! I don't believe you. I don't believe you. I can't believe you.

GLADYS:

Mama!

SABINA:

Who's that?

MRS. ANTROBUS:

That's Gladys and her baby. I don't believe you. Gladys, Sabina says the war's over. Oh, Sabina.

SABINA:

Leaning over the BABY.

Goodness! Are there any babies left in the world! Can it *see?* And can it cry and everything?

GLADYS:

Yes, he can. He notices everything very well.

SABINA:

Where on earth did you get it? Oh, I won't ask.—Lord, I've lived all these seven years around camp and I've forgotten how to behave.—Now we've got to think about the men coming home.—Mrs. Antrobus, go and wash your face, I'm ashamed of you. Put your best clothes on. Mr. Antrobus'll be here this afternoon. I just saw him downtown.

MRS. ANTROBUS AND GLADYS:

He's alive!! He'll be here!! Sabina, you're not joking?

MRS. ANTROBUS:

And Henry?

SABINA:

Drily.

Yes, Henry's alive, too, that's what they say. Now don't stop to talk. Get yourselves fixed up. Gladys, you look terrible. Have you any decent clothes?

SABINA *has pushed them toward the trapdoor.*

MRS. ANTROBUS:

Half down.

Yes, I've something to wear just for this very day. But, Sabina,— who won the war?

SABINA:

Don't stop now,—just wash your face.

A whistle sounds in the distance.

Oh, my God, what's that silly little noise?

MRS. ANTROBUS:

Why, it sounds like . . . it sounds like what used to be the noon whistle at the shoe-polish factory.

Exit.

SABINA:

That's what it is. Seems to me like peacetime's coming along pretty fast—shoe polish!

GLADYS:

Half down.

Sabina, how soon after peacetime begins does the milkman start coming to the door?

SABINA:

As soon as he catches a cow. Give him time to catch a cow, dear.

Exit GLADYS. SABINA *walks about a moment, thinking.*

Shoe polish! My, I'd forgotten what peacetime was like.

She shakes her head, then sits down by the trapdoor and starts talking down the hole.

Mrs. Antrobus, guess what I saw Mr. Antrobus doing this morning at dawn. He was tacking up a piece of paper on the door of the Town Hall. You'll die when you hear: it was a recipe for grass soup, for a grass soup that doesn't give you the diarrhea. Mr. Antrobus is still thinking up new things.—He told me to give you his love. He's got all sorts of ideas for peacetime, he says. No more laziness and idiocy, he says. And oh, yes! Where are his books? What? Well, pass them up. The first thing he wants to see are his books. He says if you've burnt those books, or if the rats have eaten them, he says it isn't worthwhile starting over again. Everybody's going to be beautiful, he says, and diligent, and very intelligent.

A hand reaches up with two volumes.

What language is that? Pu-u-gh,—mold! And he's got such plans for you, Mrs. Antrobus. You're going to study history and algebra—and so are Gladys and I—and philosophy. You should hear him talk:

Taking two more volumes.

Well, these are in English, anyway.—To hear him talk, seems like he expects you to be a combination, Mrs. Antrobus, of a saint and a college professor, and a dancehall hostess, if you know what I mean.

Two more volumes.

Ugh. German!

She is lying on the floor; one elbow bent, her cheek on her hand, meditatively.

Yes, peace will be here before we know it. In a week or two we'll be asking the Perkinses in for a quiet evening of bridge. We'll turn on the radio and hear how to be big successes with a new toothpaste. We'll trot down to the movies and see how girls with wax faces live—all *that* will begin again. Oh, Mrs. Antrobus, God forgive me but I enjoyed the war. Everybody's at their best in wartime. I'm sorry it's over. And, oh, I forgot! Mr. Antrobus sent you another message—can you hear me?—

Enter HENRY, *blackened and sullen. He is wearing torn overalls, but has one gaudy admiral's epaulette hanging by a thread from his right shoulder, and there are vestiges of gold and scarlet braid running down his left trouser leg. He stands listening.*

Listen! Henry's never to put foot in this house again, he says. He'll kill Henry on sight, if he sees him.

You don't know about Henry??? Well, where have you been? What? Well, Henry rose right to the top. Top of *what*? Listen, I'm telling you. Henry rose from corporal to captain, to major, to general.—I don't know how to say it, but the enemy is *Henry;* Henry *is* the enemy. Everybody knows that.

HENRY:
He'll kill me, will he?

SABINA:
Who are *you*? I'm not afraid of you. The war's over.

HENRY:

I'll kill him so fast. I've spent seven years trying to find him; the others I killed were just substitutes.

SABINA:

Goodness! It's Henry!—

He makes an angry gesture.

Oh, I'm not afraid of you. The war's over, Henry Antrobus, and you're not any more important than any other unemployed. You go away and hide yourself, until we calm your father down.

HENRY:

The first thing to do is to burn up those old books; it's the ideas he gets out of those old books that . . . that makes the whole world so you can't live in it.

He reels forward and starts kicking the books about, but suddenly falls down in a sitting position.

SABINA:

You leave those books alone!! Mr. Antrobus is looking forward to them a-special.—Gracious sakes, Henry, you're so tired you can't stand up. Your mother and sister'll be here in a minute and we'll think what to do about you.

HENRY:

What did they ever care about me?

SABINA:

There's that old whine again. All you people think you're not loved enough, nobody loves you. Well, you start being lovable and we'll love you.

HENRY:

Outraged.

I don't want anybody to love me.

SABINA:

Then stop talking about it all the time.

HENRY:

I *never* talk about it. The last thing I want is anybody to pay any attention to me.

SABINA:

I can hear it behind every word you say.

HENRY:

I want everybody to hate me.

SABINA:

Yes, you've decided that's second best, but it's still the same thing.—Mrs. Antrobus! Henry's here. He's so tired he can't stand up.

MRS. ANTROBUS *and* GLADYS, *with her* BABY, *emerge. They are dressed as in Act I.* MRS. ANTROBUS *carries some objects in her apron, and* GLADYS *has a blanket over her shoulder.*

MRS. ANTROBUS AND GLADYS:

Henry! Henry! Henry!

HENRY:

Glaring at them.

Have you anything to eat?

MRS. ANTROBUS:

Yes, I have, Henry. I've been saving it for this very day,—two good baked potatoes. No! Henry! one of them's for your father. Henry!! Give me that other potato back this minute.

SABINA *sidles up behind him and snatches the other potato away.*

SABINA:

He's so dog-tired he doesn't know what he's doing.

MRS. ANTROBUS:

Now you just rest there, Henry, until I can get your room ready. Eat that potato good and slow, so you can get all the nourishment out of it.

HENRY:

You all might as well know right now that I haven't come back here to live.

MRS. ANTROBUS:

Sh. . . . I'll put this coat over you. Your room's hardly damaged at all. Your football trophies are a little tarnished, but Sabina and I will polish them up tomorrow.

HENRY:

Did you hear me? I don't live here. I don't belong to anybody.

MRS. ANTROBUS:

Why, how can you say a thing like that! You certainly do belong right here. Where else would you want to go? Your forehead's feverish, Henry, seems to me. You'd better give me that gun, Henry. You won't need that any more.

GLADYS:

Whispering.

Look, he's fallen asleep already, with his potato half-chewed.

SABINA:

Puh! The terror of the world.

MRS. ANTROBUS:

Sabina, you mind your own business, and start putting the room to rights.

HENRY *has turned his face to the back of the sofa.* MRS. ANTROBUS *gingerly puts the revolver in her apron pocket, then helps* SABINA. SABINA *has found a rope hanging from the ceiling. Grunting, she hangs all her weight on it, and as she pulls the walls begin to move into their right places.* MRS. ANTROBUS *brings the over-turned tables, chairs and hassock into the positions of Act I.*

SABINA:

That's all we do—always beginning again! Over and over again. Always beginning again.

She pulls on the rope and a part of the wall moves into place. She stops. Meditatively:

How do we know that it'll be any better than before? Why do we go on pretending? Someday the whole earth's going to have to turn cold anyway, and until that time all these other things'll be happening again: it will be more wars and more walls of ice and floods and earthquakes.

MRS. ANTROBUS:

Sabina!! Stop arguing and go on with your work.

SABINA:

All right. I'll go on just out of *habit,* but I won't believe in it.

MRS. ANTROBUS:

Aroused.

Now, Sabina. I've let you talk long enough. I don't want to hear any more of it. Do I have to explain to you what everybody knows,—everybody who keeps a home going? Do I have to say to you what nobody should ever *have* to say, because they can read it in each other's eyes?

Now listen to me:

MRS. ANTROBUS *takes hold of the rope.*

I could live for seventy years in a cellar and make soup out of grass and bark, without ever doubting that this world has a work to do and will do it.

Do you hear me?

SABINA:
Frightened.

Yes, Mrs. Antrobus.

MRS. ANTROBUS:
Sabina, do you see this house,—216 Cedar Street,—do you see it?

SABINA:
Yes, Mrs. Antrobus.

MRS. ANTROBUS:
Well, just to have known this house is to have seen the idea of what we can do someday if we keep our wits about us. Too many people have suffered and died for my children for us to start reneging now. So we'll start putting this house to rights: Now, Sabina, go and see what you can do in the kitchen.

SABINA:
Kitchen! Why is it that however far I go away, I always find myself back in the kitchen?

Exit.

MRS. ANTROBUS:
Still thinking over her last speech, relaxes and says with a reminiscent smile:

Goodness gracious, wouldn't you know that my father was a parson? It was just like I heard his own voice speaking and he's been dead five thousand years. There! I've gone and almost waked Henry up.

HENRY:
Talking in his sleep, indistinctly.

Fellows . . . what have they done for us? . . . Blocked our way at every step. Kept everything in their own hands. And you've stood it. When are you going to wake up?

MRS. ANTROBUS:

Sh, Henry. Go to sleep. Go to sleep. Go to sleep.—Well, that looks better. Now let's go and help Sabina.

GLADYS:

Mama, I'm going out into the backyard and hold the baby right up in the air. And show him that we don't have to be afraid any more.

Exit GLADYS *to the kitchen.*

MRS. ANTROBUS *glances at* HENRY, *exits into kitchen.* HENRY *thrashes about in his sleep. Enter* ANTROBUS, *his arms full of bundles, chewing the end of a carrot. He has a slight limp. Over the suit of Act I he is wearing an overcoat too long for him, its skirts trailing on the ground. He lets his bundles fall and stands looking about. Presently his attention is fixed on* HENRY, *whose words grow clearer.*

HENRY:

All right! What have you got to lose? What have they done for us? That's right—nothing. Tear everything down. I don't care what you smash. We'll begin again and we'll show 'em.

ANTROBUS *takes out his revolver and holds it pointing downwards. With his back toward the audience he moves toward the footlights.*

HENRY'S *voice grows louder and he wakes with a start. They stare at one another. Then* HENRY *sits up quickly. Throughout the following scene* HENRY *is played, not as a misunderstood or misguided young man, but as a representation of strong unreconciled evil.*

All right! Do something.

Pause.

Don't think I'm afraid of you, either. All right, do what you were going to do. Do it.

Furiously.

Shoot me, I tell you. You don't have to think I'm any relation of yours. I haven't got any father or any mother, or brothers or sisters. And I don't want any. And what's more I haven't got anybody over me; and I never will have. I'm alone, and that's all I want to be: alone. So you can shoot me.

ANTROBUS:

You're the last person I wanted to see. The sight of you dries up all my plans and hopes. I wish I were back at war still, because it's easier to fight you than to live with you. War's a pleasure— do you hear me?—War's a pleasure compared to what faces us now: trying to build up a peacetime with you in the middle of it.

ANTROBUS *walks up to the window.*

HENRY:

I'm not going to be a part of any peacetime of yours. I'm going a long way from here and make my own world that's fit for a man to live in. Where a man can be free, and have a chance, and do what he wants to do in his own way.

ANTROBUS:

His attention arrested; thoughtfully. He throws the gun out of the window and turns with hope.

. . . Henry, let's try again.

HENRY:

Try what? Living *here*?—Speaking polite downtown to all the old men like you? Standing like a sheep at the street corner until the red light turns to green? Being a good boy and a good sheep, like all the stinking ideas you get out of your books? Oh, no. I'll make a world, and I'll show you.

ANTROBUS:
Hard.

How can you make a world for people to live in, unless you've first put order in yourself? Mark my words: I shall continue fighting you until my last breath as long as you mix up your idea of liberty with your idea of hogging everything for yourself. I shall have no pity on you. I shall pursue you to the far corners of the earth. You and I want the same thing; but until you think of it as something that everyone has a right to, you are my deadly enemy and I will destroy you.—I hear your mother's voice in the kitchen. Have you seen her?

HENRY:
I have no mother. Get it into your head. I don't belong here. I have nothing to do here. I have no home.

ANTROBUS:
Then why did you come here? With the whole world to choose from, why did you come to this one place: 216 Cedar Street, Excelsior, New Jersey. . . . Well?

HENRY:
What if I did? What if I wanted to look at it once more, to see if—

ANTROBUS:
Oh, you're related, all right—When your mother comes in you must behave yourself. Do you hear me?

HENRY:
Wildly.

What is this?—*must behave* yourself. Don't you say *must* to me.

ANTROBUS:

Quiet!

Enter MRS. ANTROBUS *and* SABINA.

HENRY:

Nobody can say *must* to me. All my life everybody's been crossing me,—everybody, everything, all of you. I'm going to be free,
even if I have to kill half the world for it. Right now, too. Let me
get my hands on his throat. I'll show him.

He advances toward ANTROBUS. *Suddenly,* SABINA *jumps
between them and calls out in her own person:*

SABINA:

Stop! Stop! Don't play this scene. You know what happened last
night. Stop the play.

The men fall back, panting. HENRY *covers his face with his
hands.*

Last night you almost strangled him. You became a regular sav-
age. Stop it!

HENRY:

It's true. I'm sorry. I don't know what comes over me. I have
nothing against him personally. I respect him very much . . .
I . . . I admire him. But something comes over me. It's like I
become fifteen years old again. I . . . I . . . listen: my own father
used to whip me and lock me up every Saturday night. I never
had enough to eat. He never let me have enough money to buy
decent clothes. I was ashamed to go downtown. I never could
go to the dances. My father and my uncle put rules in the way of
everything I wanted to do. They tried to prevent my living at
all.—I'm sorry. I'm sorry.

MRS. ANTROBUS:

Quickly.

No, go on. Finish what you were saying. Say it all.

HENRY:

In this scene it's as though I were back in High School again. It's like I had some big emptiness inside me,—the emptiness of being hated and blocked at every turn. And the emptiness fills up with the one thought that you have to strike and fight and kill. Listen, it's as though you have to kill somebody else so as not to end up killing yourself.

SABINA:

That's not true. I knew your father and your uncle and your mother. You imagined all that. Why, they did everything they could for you. How can you say things like that? They didn't lock you up.

HENRY:

They did. They did. They wished I hadn't been born.

SABINA:

That's not true.

ANTROBUS:

In his own person, with self-condemnation, but cold and proud.

Wait a minute. I have something to say, too. It's not wholly his fault that he wants to strangle me in this scene. It's my fault, too. He wouldn't feel that way unless there were something in me that reminded him of all that. He talks about an emptiness. Well, there's an emptiness in me, too. Yes,—work, work, work,— that's all I do. I've ceased to *live*. No wonder he feels that anger coming over him.

MRS. ANTROBUS:

There! At least you've said it.

SABINA:

We're all just as wicked as we can be, and that's the God's truth.

MRS. ANTROBUS:

Nods a moment, then comes forward; quietly:

Come. Come and put your head under some cold water.

SABINA:

In a whisper.

I'll go with him. I've known him a long while. You have to go on with the play. Come with me.

HENRY *starts out with* SABINA, *but turns at the exit and says to* ANTROBUS:

HENRY:

Thanks. Thanks for what you said. I'll be all right tomorrow. I won't lose control in that place. I promise.

Exeunt HENRY *and* SABINA.

ANTROBUS *starts toward the front door, fastens it.*

MRS. ANTROBUS: *goes up stage and places the chair close to table.*

MRS. ANTROBUS:

George, do I see you limping?

ANTROBUS:

Yes, a little. My old wound from the other war started smarting again. I can manage.

MRS. ANTROBUS:

Looking out of the window.

Some lights are coming on,—the first in seven years. People are walking up and down looking at them. Over in Hawkins' open lot they've built a bonfire to celebrate the peace. They're dancing around it like scarecrows.

ANTROBUS:

A bonfire! As though they hadn't seen enough things burning.—Maggie,—the dog died?

MRS. ANTROBUS:

Oh, yes. Long ago. There are no dogs left in Excelsior.—You're back again! All these years. I gave up counting on letters. The few that arrived were anywhere from six months to a year late.

ANTROBUS:

Yes, the ocean's full of letters, along with the other things.

MRS. ANTROBUS:

George, sit down, you're tired.

ANTROBUS:

No, you sit down. I'm tired but I'm restless.

Suddenly, as she comes forward:

Maggie! I've lost it. I've lost it.

MRS. ANTROBUS:

What, George? What have you lost?

ANTROBUS:

The most important thing of all: The desire to begin again, to start building.

MRS. ANTROBUS:

Sitting in the chair right of the table.

Well, it will come back.

ANTROBUS:

At the window.

I've lost it. This minute I feel like all those people dancing around the bonfire—just relief. Just the desire to settle down; to slip into the old grooves and keep the neighbors from walking over my lawn.—Hm. But during the war,—in the middle of all that blood and dirt and hot and cold—every day and night, I'd have moments, Maggie, when I *saw* the things that we could do when it was over. When you're at war you think about a better life; when you're at peace you think about a more comfortable one. I've lost it. I feel sick and tired.

MRS. ANTROBUS:
Listen! The baby's crying.

I hear Gladys talking. Probably she's quieting Henry again. George, while Gladys and I were living here—like moles, like rats, and when we were at our wits' end to save the baby's life— the only thought we clung to was that you were going to bring something good out of this suffering. In the night, in the dark, we'd whisper about it, starving and sick.—Oh, George, you'll have to get it back again. Think! What else kept us alive all these years? Even now, it's not comfort we want. We can suffer whatever's necessary; only give us back that promise.

Enter SABINA *with a lighted lamp. She is dressed as in Act I.*

SABINA:
Mrs. Antrobus . . .

MRS. ANTROBUS:
Yes, Sabina?

SABINA:
Will you need me?

MRS. ANTROBUS:
No, Sabina, you can go to bed.

SABINA:
Mrs. Antrobus, if it's all right with you, I'd like to go to the bonfire and celebrate seeing the war's over. And, Mrs. Antrobus,

they've opened the Gem Movie Theatre and they're giving away a hand-painted soup tureen to every lady, and I thought one of us ought to go.

ANTROBUS:

Well, Sabina, I haven't any money. I haven't seen any money for quite a while.

SABINA:

Oh, you don't need money. They're taking anything you can give them. And I have some . . . some . . . Mrs. Antrobus, promise you won't tell anyone. It's a little against the law. But I'll give you some, too.

ANTROBUS:

What is it?

SABINA:

I'll give you some, too. Yesterday I picked up a lot of . . . of beef-cubes!

MRS. ANTROBUS *turns and says calmly:*

MRS. ANTROBUS:

But, Sabina, you know you ought to give that in to the Center downtown. They know who needs them most.

SABINA:

Outburst.

Mrs. Antrobus, I didn't make this war. I didn't ask for it. And, in my opinion, after anybody's gone through what we've gone through, they have a right to grab what they can find. You're a very nice man, Mr. Antrobus, but you'd have got on better in the world if you'd realized that dog-eat-dog was the rule in the beginning and always will be. And most of all now.

In tears.

Oh, the world's an awful place, and you know it is. I used to think something could be done about it; but I know better now. I hate it. I hate it.

She comes forward slowly and brings six cubes from the bag.

All right. All right. You can have them.

ANTROBUS:
Thank you, Sabina.

SABINA:
Can I have . . . can I have one to go to the movies?

ANTROBUS *in silence gives her one.*

Thank you.

ANTROBUS:
Good night, Sabina.

SABINA:
Mr. Antrobus, don't mind what I say. I'm just an ordinary girl, you know what I mean, I'm just an ordinary girl. But you're a bright man, you're a very bright man, and of course you invented the alphabet and the wheel, and, my God, a lot of things . . . and if you've got any other plans, my God, don't let me upset them. Only every now and then I've got to go to the movies. I mean my nerves can't stand it. But if you have any ideas about improving the crazy old world, I'm really with you. I really am. Because it's . . . it's . . . Good night.

She goes out. ANTROBUS *starts laughing softly with exhilaration.*

ANTROBUS:
Now I remember what three things always went together when I was able to see things most clearly: three things. Three things:

He points to where SABINA *has gone out.*

The voice of the people in their confusion and their need. And the thought of you and the children and this house. And . . . Maggie! I didn't dare ask you: my books! They haven't been lost, have they?

MRS. ANTROBUS:

No. There are some of them right here. Kind of tattered. ·

ANTROBUS:

Yes.—Remember, Maggie, we almost lost them once before? And when we finally did collect a few torn copies out of old cellars they ran in everyone's head like a fever. They as good as rebuilt the world.

Pauses, book in hand, and looks up.

Oh, I've never forgotten for long at a time that living is struggle. I know that every good and excellent thing in the world stands moment by moment on the razor-edge of danger and must be fought for—whether it's a field, or a home, or a country. All I ask is the chance to build new worlds and God has always given us that. And has given us

Opening the book

voices to guide us; and the memory of our mistakes to warn us. Maggie, you and I will remember in peacetime all the resolves that were so clear to us in the days of war. We've come a long ways. We've learned. We're learning. And the steps of our journey are marked for us here.

He stands by the table turning the leaves of a book.

Sometimes out there in the war,—standing all night on a hill—I'd try and remember some of the words in these books. Parts of them and phrases would come back to me. And after a while I used to give names to the hours of the night.

He sits, hunting for a passage in the book.

Nine o'clock I used to call Spinoza. Where is it: "After experience had taught me—"

The back wall has disappeared, revealing the platform. FRED BAILEY *carrying his numeral has started from left to right.* MRS. ANTROBUS *sits by the table sewing.*

BAILEY:

"After experience had taught me that the common occurrences of daily life are vain and futile; and I saw that all the objects of my desire and fear were in themselves nothing good nor bad save insofar as the mind was affected by them; I at length determined to search out whether there was something truly good and communicable to man."

Almost without break HESTER, *carrying a large Roman numeral ten, starts crossing the platform.* GLADYS *appears at the kitchen door and moves toward her mother's chair.*

HESTER:

"Then tell me, O Critias, how will a man choose the ruler that shall rule over him? Will he not choose a man who has first established order in himself, knowing that any decision that has its spring from anger or pride or vanity can be multiplied a thousand fold in its effects upon the citizens?"

HESTER *disappears and* IVY, *as eleven o'clock starts speaking.*

IVY:

"This good estate of the mind possessing its object in energy we call divine. This we mortals have occasionally and it is this energy which is pleasantest and best. But God has it always. It is wonderful in us; but in Him how much more wonderful."

As MR. TREMAYNE *starts to speak,* HENRY *appears at the edge of the scene, brooding and unreconciled, but present.*

TREMAYNE:

"In the beginning, God created the Heavens and the earth; And the Earth was waste and void; And the darkness was upon the face of the deep. And the Lord said let there be light and there was light."

Sudden black-out and silence, except for the last strokes of the midnight bell. Then just as suddenly the lights go up, and SABINA *is standing at the window, as at the opening of the play.*

SABINA:

Oh, oh, oh. Six o'clock and the master not home yet. Pray God nothing serious has happened to him crossing the Hudson River. But I wouldn't be surprised. The whole world's at sixes and sevens, and why the house hasn't fallen down about our ears long ago is a miracle to me.

She comes down to the footlights.

This is where you came in. We have to go on for ages and ages yet.

You go home.

The end of this play isn't written yet.

Mr. and Mrs. Antrobus! Their heads are full of plans and they're as confident as the first day they began,—and they told me to tell you: good night.

Afterword

Overview

Thornton Wilder began writing *The Skin of Our Teeth* (then titled *The Ends of the Worlds*) on June 24, 1940, at the MacDowell Colony, the artists and writers retreat in Peterborough, New Hampshire, where *Our Town* had been born three years earlier. He was searching for a way to bear witness to a world increasingly at war, and he had been inspired, in part, by the way James Joyce had presented "ancient man as an ever-present double to modern man" in *Finnegans Wake*. Wilder coupled this note in his journal entry of July 6, 1940, with these quasi-hopeful words: "During the last year subject after subject presented itself and crumbled away in my hands. Can this one hold out?" Hold out it did, although not without many discouraging and—appropriately for the property—dramatic moments.

During a nearly three-month stay that fall at the Château Frontenac in Quebec, a still deeper retreat from places where people knew him, Wilder completed much of the work on the first two acts. Significantly, he was now living among people who were officially at war. On November 13, he wrote his dramatic agent: "Scarcely dare talk about it; looks to me like the play's prodigious. First two acts done. Not a sight or sound out of me until I return with the finished script, maybe as soon as Dec. 10."

He did not meet his deadline. On December 14, about to leave Quebec, Wilder wrote Robert Ardrey, a fellow playwright and his former student, "The new play is not finished yet after all. Heigh-ho. I swear I don't know what I've got here. I just keep trying to bring into shape—it a fine idea, but very hard to do."

In the end, Act III, the war act, which Wilder found the most difficult to write, was not ready for Jed Harris, his director of choice, until January 1, 1942, a year later. Many honorable deeds and distractions came between Wilder and his goal of completing the play, among them a three-month trip on a cultural goodwill mission to Latin America for the Department of State, a summer term teaching a double course load at the University of Chicago, and an autumn trip to London as U.S. delegate to an international PEN conference. This last assignment offered him an opportunity to view actual war damage and to talk with courageous civilians, soldiers, and fighter and bomber pilots in England and Scotland. These encounters helped Wilder to begin to conceive for the end of the play a note about the survival of the human race that would be hopeful but not "trite" or "evasive," words he used at the time. His search for the right words continued during the play's rehearsal period until, as a last touch, he added George Antrobus's final speech in the play: "We've come a long ways. We've learned. We're learning. . . ."

Several years later, in a 1948 letter to his brother, Amos, Wilder recalled this creative challenge:

> I've always assumed a very slow curve of civilization. But I always affirm too that my toleration of humanity's failings is more affirmative than most "optimists." When I first

wrote *Skin of Our Teeth* it lacked that motto-humanity-
climbing-upward speeches of Mr. Antrobus at the end. I
assumed that they were omnipresent in the play and didn't
have to be stated. I assumed that they were self-evident,—
that's how highly I believed in mankind. But more and
more of the early readers found the play "defeatist." So I
wrote in the moral and crossed the t's and i's.

It was Wilder's expectation that Jed Harris, who had produced and directed *Our Town*, would play the same roles for *The
Skin of Our Teeth*. Harris turned him down, however. Wilder
then offered the producer's role to Michael Myerberg, an entertainment promoter who had worked as Leopold Stokowski's
manager. Wilder had known Myerberg casually for about five
years, and did not consider his lack of Broadway experience a
disadvantage. On the contrary, he made this unusual choice
because he had no faith that, with the exception of the legendary
Harris, any experienced Broadway producer could do justice to a
drama that Wilder predicted to his attorney would "probably
involve a complicated history." He was right.

Exuding just the fresh energy that Wilder was counting on,
Myerberg orchestrated a production that included the exciting
young director, Elia Kazan, and a galaxy of distinguished actors:
Fredric March and Florence Eldridge as Mr. and Mrs. Antrobus;
Montgomery Clift and Frances Heflin as Henry and Gladys; Florence Reed as the Fortune Teller; and the already legendary Tallulah Bankhead as Sabina. But almost immediately there were
complications. Myerberg's imperiousness, unpredictable moods,
and indifference in handling budgets and people combined with
Bankhead's volatile temperament to make life unusually hellish
for the cast as well as the author and his representatives.

Bad feeling backstage did not at first compromise the quality
of the production. *Skin* played to mostly favorable press and

many a sold-out house in its four-week, four-city tryout period in New Haven, Baltimore, Philadelphia, and Washington, D.C. Not that people necessarily understood a play that an out-of-town *Variety* story reported "bewilders, bemuses and befuddles while it amuses." Had the reporter added the word "upsets" to the list, he would have scooped Wilder's own assessment, written to his family soon after rehearsals had begun: "I think it's a very good play, but it's so daringly written as to theatre-mood that it may well puzzle and upset instead of amuse and move."

And upset it did. As long as there is Broadway lore, it will likely include stories of taxis lining up early to snag the fares of people fleeing *The Skin of Our Teeth* at the end of Act I or II, some even jamming their fists through the play's posters along the way. According to Richard Maney, the play's publicist, fifteen people walked out early at the world premiere in New Haven's Shubert Theater on October 15, 1942. Hoping that knowledge might stem the tide, Myerberg ordered Maney to write a synopsis of the play to insert in the playbill. These words greeted the audience at the second performance:

The Skin of Our Teeth is a comedy about George Antrobus, his wife and two children, and their general utility maid, Lily Sabina, all of Exelsior, New Jersey. George Antrobus is John Doe or George Spelvin or you—the average American at grips with destiny, sometimes sour, sometimes sweet. The Antrobuses have survived fire, flood, pestilence, the seven-year locusts, the ice age, the black pox and the double feature, a dozen wars and as many depressions. They have run many a gamut, are as durable as radiators, and look upon the future with a disarming optimism. Alternately bewitched, befuddled and becalmed, they are the stuff of which heroes are made—heroes and buffoons. They are true offspring of Adam and Eve, victims of all the ills that flesh is heir to. They have survived a thousand calamities by the skin of their teeth, and Mr. Wilder's play is a tribute to their indestructibility.

Out-of-town success is no guarantee of Broadway success, but in the case of *Skin,* which opened on November 18 at the Plymouth Theater in New York, it was. With few exceptions, reviews were strong, some even raves: "A dramatic bombshell"—*Life;* "Theater-going became a rare and electrifying experience"—*New York Herald Tribune;* "Quite sure to prove the supreme novelty of the theater season"—*New York Daily News.* Two especially influential tastemakers put the case this way: "One of the wisest and friskiest comedies written in a long time," critic Brooks Atkinson wrote in the *New York Times.* Wilder's friend, the critic and commentator Alexander Woollcott, called *The Skin of Our Teeth* "the nearest thing to a great play which the American theater has yet produced." There were critics on the other side of the fence, of course. As a general comment, they found tricks rather than substance. "[It] dolls up its theme rather than dramatizes it," said *Time.* "It is too overt, too garish, too sensational in the literal sense," wrote the *Commonweal* reviewer.

At the end of a theatrical day, the box office never lies. Through the first five months of the run, *The Skin of Our Teeth* rarely earned less than $20,000 a week in ticket sales, all but a sellout. After falling off only a bit (to the $16,000 to $18,000 range) in the normally slower theatrical months of March and April, sales jumped up again when the play was awarded the Pulitzer Prize for Drama in May 1943.

Controversy is always good for box office. Consequently, it did not hurt sales when Henry Morton Robinson and Joseph Campbell, students of James Joyce, ignited a firestorm of debate and comment in the press when they accused Wilder in two articles published in *The Saturday Review of Literature* in December 1942 and January 1943, of writing "an Americanized recreation, thinly disguised," based on Joyce's *Finnegans Wake*. The accusers never used the word "plagiarism," but they implied it, and the term appeared in the press. Specious if malicious, the charge was dismissed by authorities at the time and since. Still, it probably cost *The Skin of Our Teeth* the 1943 Drama Critics Award, but not the Pulitzer Prize. At the time, Wilder chose not to respond publicly to the charges, other than to encourage those interested to embark on the daunting task of reading *Finnegans Wake* and deciding for themselves.

Wilder was, in fact, in no position to give serious attention to his accusers even if he had wanted to. Two months before the play went into rehearsal, at age forty-five, he had eagerly entered active duty with Army Air Force Intelligence, turning over the playwright's duties to his agent, his attorney, and his knowledgeable sister, Isabel, a graduate of the Yale School of Drama.

Nevertheless, until the recently promoted Major Wilder departed for overseas duty in North Africa in late May 1943, he found it impossible to avoid all the drama playing out on both sides of the curtain. Through letters, telegrams, occasional visits from various principals, and anguished phone calls, Wilder found himself dragged into the fray surrounding *The Skin of Our Teeth*. He saw the show from beginning to end only twice, once in November just before the New York opening, and again in April 1943.

Had the original cast held on, *Skin* might well have played far longer on Broadway than it did. But by June 1943, backstage tensions had become so intolerable that March, Eldridge, and Bankhead took advantage of clauses in their contracts and left the show. Like a wounded animal, *Skin* (now earning $10,000 or less weekly at the box office) limped through the always difficult summer months with new faces in key roles. As the production had come to depend on Tallulah Bankhead's star power in the role of Sabina, her departure was all but a death blow.

A play as famous and even infamous as *The Skin of Our Teeth* could usually count on a successful post-Broadway national tour, and Myerberg planned this for the fall, starting with a two-week engagement in Boston. The 359-performance Broadway run closed on Saturday, September 25, opened in Boston the following Monday and closed after only the first week. Gladys George, the new Sabina, was now out of the part, claiming throat problems. She was replaced by Elizabeth Scott. The box office was terrible. This "sudden eclipse," wrote a *Variety* reporter, "was no surprise to those who have followed the vagaries of the show."

A by-product of *Skin*'s early demise was the earlier-than-anticipated release of the amateur and stock rights and the beginning, in 1944, of *Skin*'s enduring popularity with high school, college, and community drama groups. Nor has the play faded entirely from the professional stages. Since 1980, it has been produced some twenty times in stock and regional theaters around the country. Major productions since the war have included the 1955 revival starring Mary Martin and Helen Hayes and the 1961 ANTA–American Repertory Company revival. Both productions were sent abroad as part of the State Department's cultural programming. (The 1955 *Skin*, directed by Alan Schneider, went to Paris, while the 1961 production played in twenty-four countries in Europe and Latin America.) In 1975, José Quintero directed a production that kicked off the American Bicentennial Theater season project at the John F. Kennedy Center for the Performing Arts in Washington with Elizabeth Ashley as Sabina. *Skin* had its last New York appearance in 1998. The production, by the New York Shakespeare Festival in its Delacorte Theater in Central Park, was directed by Irene Lewis and featured Kristen Johnson as Sabina. In 1945, Laurence Olivier directed the London opening with his wife, Vivien Leigh, as Sabina; no British production is more famous. Finally, not to be forgotten are Wilder's own appearances playing George Antrobus in several summer stock productions after

World War II, including such notable "straw hat" addresses as the Berkshire Festival Playhouse in Stockbridge, the South Shore Players in Cohasset, Massachusetts, and the historic Westport Country Playhouse in Westport, Connecticut.

There have been several televised versions of *The Skin of Our Teeth*, including a 1952 Pulitzer Prize Playhouse production on which Wilder himself consulted. None is better remembered today than the Globe Theater's important 1983 PBS "American Playhouse" version. But like a mountain that refuses to be conquered, the play has so far resisted all attempts to be adapted as a major film, opera, or musical. The prospect has attracted the attention of such talents as Leonard Bernstein, Mary Ellen Bute, Katharine Hepburn, Spencer Tracy—and most recently, John Kander, Fred Ebb, and Joe Stein. The story of *Skin* in translation is a different matter. Starting with a performance in German in Zurich's renowned Schauspielhaus in the spring of 1944, *The Skin of Our Teeth* has been performed in some twenty languages in more than forty countries. As Wilder noted in his influential preface to *Three Plays* (1957), it had a special resonance in postwar Germany, where the first production occurred in the ruins of Darmstadt on March 31, 1946. By November 1949, *Skin* had been performed in both the Eastern and Western Zones 501 times by fifteen companies in thirty German cities. (By the late 1940s, Wilder's works, including *Skin*, had been banned in the Soviet Union and most Eastern bloc countries, including East Germany, for promoting bourgeois values.) In short, *The Skin of Our Teeth*—so often thought of as especially American because of its eagerness, high jinks, and vision of human capability—is a well-established piece of world theater, although it would also be fair to say that it has been produced less frequently since the end of the Cold War.

The experimental techniques Wilder employed in 1942—the anachronisms, the asides, the interruptions—are now familiar to a twenty-first-century audience raised on modern theater and the television sitcom. And contemporary critics have squirmed in their seats at Wilder's proclamations about patriotism and loyalty and what one admirer of the play in 1975 summarized as a perceived tendency toward "excessively abstract, dreamy allegory, populated by stock characters of popular cliché." Have the novelty of the play and its whimsy grown thin for some theatergoers? Perhaps. But what the record also shows is that because of its theatricality and humor, and the sheer craziness of exploring and producing what is known in the business as a "theatrical bible," *The Skin of Our Teeth* continues to attract and to hold the attention of actors, audiences, playwrights, and students today, more than sixty years after it opened on Broadway.

—Tappan Wilder

Chevy Chase, Maryland

Readings

During the Writing of the Play

A Letter

Wilder writes a newsy letter, from which this excerpt is taken, to his family from the Château Frontenac.

Sunday, Oct. 20, 1940, 11:10 P.M.

Chateau Frontenac

Quebec, P.Q.

Dear Ones:

The first snow. And a surprise. I'd just—but I'd better tell you the whole afternoon.

After lunch, it being a fine day I thought I'd get out the car, just to keep my hand in. So I drove all around the Ile d'Orleans, the farms pretty well modernized, but great views of the great river and many yellow-ochre forests. Then I drove to the Falls of Montmorency—one hundred feet higher than Niagara, and a very fine sight. (Coleridge—I think it's Coleridge—"uses" them in a poem in that "Spirit of Man" anthology on your table there.) The water hurtles down creating a wide diversity of effects in lace and mist and rainbows and parsley-sprays and gossamer ladders and climbing serpents. And I had tea at a very nice hotel beside it, now unfortunately closed to residence, called Kent House, because it was the summer house of the Duke of Kent, Father of Queen Victoria, then Governor-General of New France.

Then I got home and went to church to Vespers at St. Matthew's, which on All Soul's Day—November first, as all readers of *Finnegans Wake* must know well—will celebrate its mere 150th anniversary, which must arouse a scornful laugh from the Roman Catholic churches, all fifty of them, nearby. Half the congregation was in uniform, and we prayed for the Royal Family, and sang "God Save the King," and the Rector cast some of those condescending bathetic references to our dear boys in the service which would make a conscientious objector out of a Theodore Roosevelt.

Then I stopped for something to eat in town, knowing the worst, for the food in this city is so dreadful that when I eat anywhere except in this hotel I am indubitably poisoned and belch darkly throughout the night. Then I came home to couch on paper the new suggestions for Act Two that had arrived to me during Vespers—your church-going being a lively incentive to your playwriting, though the *point-de-départ* is left far behind. On my door I found word that a special delivery was waiting for me below. It seemed impossible that you could have already received and replied To my Special, and yet you're the only correspondent whom I told my address. I thought I had turned in for the night, but just before I went below to claim the letter I looked out of the window at my now cherished view and saw Everything Covered with Snow. Well, the first snow of the year is one of my fêtes, and I had always felt that Quebec, like Litchfield, and Oxford, and, I assume, Prague, mutely *waits* for snow. So I put on my overshoes—packed, remember? at the last moment, and have taken another walk. . . .

A Journal Entry

Wilder writes in his journal about the problems he continues to face in completing Act III, in which he wished to employ a device he first used in his one-act play *Pullman Car Hiawatha* in 1931. He wrote this entry on December 2, 1941, while visiting Alexander Woollcott's retreat on Neshobe Island in Vermont.

Again bogged down and frightened. Last month in New Haven not only did I tighten up Acts One and Two—I think I can say that with the exception of a short passage in Act Two they are finished, and good—but I wrote a "through" Third Act; but it is not right.

The employment of the "Pullman Car Hiawatha" material [in *Pullman Car Hiawatha*, published in the volume *The Long Christmas Dinner and Other Plays in One Act* (1931), minutes appear as gossips, hours as philosophers, and years as theologians] is (1) Dragged in indigestibly; (2) Insufficiently related to the surrounding material; (3) An incorrect statement of the central intention of the Act—is *that* intention, by the way, to be "save the cultural tradition?"—and (4) It smacks of the *faux-sublime.*

To go back to first principles: what does one offer the audience as explanation of man's endurance, aim, and consolation? Hitherto, I had planned here to say that the existence of his children and the inventive activity of his mind keep urging him to continued and better-adjusted survival. In the Third Act I was planning to say that the ideas contained in the great books of his predecessors hang above him in mid-air furnishing him adequate direction and stimulation.

(1) Do I believe this?
(2) Have I found the correct theatrical statement for it?
(3) Is it sufficient climax for the play?

Taking these in turn: (1) I do believe it. I think the only trouble with it is that *there* is the point where the vast majority of writers hitherto would have planted the religious note. It's not so much that I deny that religious note as that it presents itself to me only intermittently and in terms too individualistic to enter the framework of this place.

(2) The statement that the ideas and books of the masters are the motive forces for man's progress is a difficult one to represent theatrically. The drawbacks against the "Pullman Car Hiawatha" treatment are that (a) the Hours-as-Philosophers runs the danger of being a cute fantasy and not a living striking metaphor, and (b) . . . I cannot find citations from the philosophers' works that briefly and succinctly express what I need here.

At all events, I have begun work as usual by excision. Out go the "people who had died in the house"—we have had enough of the common men who preceded our Antrobuses. Out also goes, I think, the natural history, though maybe that might be useful, not as giving the arch of the natural world that surrounds us, but as making more easy the identification of Stars and Hours with

Philosophers and Artists. Out go the allusions to the various calendars—partly because it is so difficult to choose *one day* to cite. Into the earlier part of the Act should go, if I can keep Hours-Philosophers, much more reference to Mr. Antrobus's books.

Couldn't the quarrel between Henry and his father hang on Henry's contempt for the books that had led his father astray?

A Country at War

After returning from a monthlong trip to England in the fall of 1941, which took him from London to Bristol and Glasgow, Wilder spoke of his impressions on NBC Radio and wrote them in an article entitled "After a Visit to England" in *The Yale Review*, from which this excerpt is taken.

At times I felt like some passerby who has strayed by accident upon a stage where a play is in progress. Each of the highly dramatic episodes of the action was clear to me, but seemed to be misunderstood by the performers. Suddenly, however, I realized that I was a late arrival; that earlier in the play there had been a scene exhibiting these characters in some situation of a gravity so profound that there was no need to allude to it afterward; that allusion could only be inadequate, so it could only be disruptive. Back had flowed the spirit of the daily life, and only with close attention could the newcomer surprise some exchange between them of glance or gesture that recalled the vows they had taken and the agony they had shared. . . .

To overemphasize a few of such difficulties—common enough to other countries even when there is no confusion of crisis to complicate them—would be an injustice to the total magnificent achievement of civilian defense in

Britain under the unheard-of conditions of the air raids. Yet to pass them over in silence would be to overlook an important new element in current attitudes. The principal thing in the mental temper of Britain is the unity and resolution exemplified in the self-imposed restraint and the co-operation of all citizens in the emergency. In a factory which produces certain delicate instruments for airplanes the workers had denied themselves three week-ends off in succession. Great was the anticipation for the recess finally accorded them. On the Friday before it they were called together at the noon hour and addressed by two air pilots each of whom had made over thirty flights into enemy territory. The airmen explained to them the urgency of the demand for the several hundred instruments that would be lost through the closing of the factory and asked them to remain at their tasks. The workers remained. On an historic estate in Sussex, a lady from Mayfair had herself milked the cow, churned the butter, and, with the help of one friend, cooked the dinner for six.

The enemy had first shown what a total war can be— every citizen bent to an activity directed against every citizen in the enemy country. Britain is making it clear that what the Germans have effected, first with rhetorical oratory, and finally with threats and coercion, a democracy can achieve with composure and free will.

Seeing His Play

After seeing *Skin* in November 1942, shortly before it opened in New York, Wilder, now an Air Force Intelligence officer, sent notes, through his dramatic agent, Harold Freedman, on the performance to Michael Myerberg (producer), Elia ("Gadgett") Kazan (director), and his sister, Isabel (his representative). His report, from which this excerpt is taken, was mailed from Spokane, Washington, November 24, 1942.

Notes on the performance of *The Skin of Our Teeth,* (Harold, will you ask a secretary to type these out and provide copies for Michael, Gadgett and my sister, as I cannot take the time to write them separately.)

First place,—many thanks to all concerned for all the fine things about the performance. The following is a list of passages that I feel would be bettered, but that doesn't mean that I am not overwhelmingly grateful for what is already there.

For me the only real flaw in the present production is the hurry-hurry-hurry. The lack of variation in pace, in the First Act, from the time of Mr. Antrobus's entrance. This uniform onward rush prevents both the serious aspect of the play emerging (so necessary as preparation for the change of tone in Act III) and prevents a real sense of excitement in the possibility of danger before the oncoming ice.

Examples: The monotonous busy-busyness of the stage pace prevents any attention being given to Mrs. Antrobus' "No, they've been as good as gold—haven't had to raise my voice once"; to the interchange between Mr. and Mrs. A while he is playing with the animals. (Keep that mammoth quiet in many places,—he's the kind that will get worse and worse.) That conversation should have ominous weight, real pauses, and much violence at its climax— "The Sun's growing cold. What can I do about that?"

Also give Mr. A. a real moment with his—"Yes, any booby can play it with it now, etc." inward, withdrawn, brooding.

The "Abel—my son—my son—Abel"—I beg you to go back to my original stage direction—she rises, sits again, rises . . . give the actors time to extract the maximum legitimate effect from these things.

Henry comes down the stairs with chairs or whatever it is and causes distraction at a vital moment.

Freddie does both his moment of despair in the chair and his Build up the Fire superbly, but it would be still stronger if the momentum about him had not been so rat-tat-tat uniform. Urge him to prepare the moments with even longer pauses, if he likes.

As Arthur Hopkins [a producer and director who admired the play and knew Wilder] said at the end of the First Act—"It's as though they had no faith in the play"— galloping as though the most they could hope for was the collection of a few laughs.

Controversy: The Playwright Finally Speaks

When Joseph Campbell and Henry Morton Robinson leveled their charges, Wilder was an acknowledged authority on Joyce's *Finnegans Wake* and his expertise in deciphering it was widely known in literary circles. Here in its entirety is the letter he wrote but did not send to the editor of *The Saturday Review of Literature* at the time of the first article, believing his rebuttal would only lead to further accusations and debate. The letter was found in Wilder's legal files and first published in 1999.

To the Editor of the Saturday Review of Literature.

Dear Sir:

Many thanks for your telephone call and your request that I comment upon the article in the Review pointing out some real and some imagined resemblances between my play, *The Skin of Our Teeth*, and James Joyce's novel, *Finnegans Wake*.

At the time I was absorbed in deciphering Joyce's novel the idea came to me that one aspect of it might be expressed in drama: the method of representing mankind's long history through superimposing different epochs of time simultaneously. I even made sketches employing Joyce's characters and locale, but soon abandoned the project. The slight element of plot in the novel is so dimly glimpsed amid the distortions of nightmare and the polyglot distortions of language that any possibility of dramatization is out of the question. The notion of a play about mankind and the family viewed through several simultaneous layers of time, however, persisted and began to surround itself with many inventions of my own. If one subject is man and the family considered historically, the element of myth inevitably presents itself. It is not necessary to go to Joyce's novel to find the motive of Adam, Eve, Cain, Abel, Lilith and Noah.

From Joyce, however, I received the idea of presenting ancient man as an ever present double to modern man. The four fundamental aspects of *Finnegans Wake* were not to my purpose and are not present in my play. Joyce's novel is primarily a study of Original Sin and the role it plays in the life of the conscience. Its recurrent motto is St. Augustine's *"O felix culpa!"* Nor could I use its secondary subject, the illustration of Vico's theory of the cyclic seasonal repetitions of human culture. Nor could I find any place for its primary literary intention, the extraordinary means Joyce found for representing the thoughts of the mind while asleep, the famous "night-language." Nor could I employ his secondary literary intention, the technical tours-de-force whereby through puns and slips of the tongue he was able to represent several layers of mental activity going on at the same time and often contradictory to one another. If I had been able to transfer to the stage several or any one of these four basic aspects of the book, wherein its greatness lies, I would have done it and would have gladly published the obligation at every step of the way.

The germ of my play, once started, began to collect about it many aspects which had nothing to do with Joyce. It fixed its thoughts on the War and the situation of the eternal family under successive catastrophes. It grouped to find a way to express dramatically the thought that the great "unread" classics furnish daily support and stimulation even to people who do not read them. But principally the play moved into its own independent existence through its insistence on being theatre, and theatre to such an extent that content was continually in danger of being overwhelmed by sheer theatric contrivances. I can think of no novel in all literature that is farther removed from theatre than *Finnegans Wake*.

The writers of the article in the *Review* list a long series of resemblances. Only those who have pored over the novel can realize how patiently the authors must have searched through that amorphous dream texture to assemble them and how surprising it is to find them confronting the concrete theatrical material they are supposed to parallel. Maggie Earwicker's letter buried in the rubbish heap behind her house becomes the letter of proud and indignant self-justification that Maggie Antrobus throws into the sea over the heads of the audience? Well, all the Margarets in the world can be presumed to have written letters that were important to them. In the most wonderful chapter in the novel, Anna Livia Plurabelle, river and woman, looks for a match to search for some peat to warm her husband's supper. The authors of the article quote this passage and tell your readers that it resembles Mrs. Antrobus and Sabina asking for fuel to warm the household against the approaching glacier. By such devices your authors could derive "Junior Miss" from *Lady Chatterley's Lover*. The ant-like industry of pedants, collecting isolated fragments, has mistaken the nature of literary influence since the first critics arose to regard books as a branch of merchandise instead of as expressions of energy.

Should a group of men of letters represent to me that the dependence of my play on Joyce's novel is so close as to justify adding a note of acknowledgment to the theatre program, I would willingly accede to their opinion. I have placed such a note twice before—once in *The Woman of Andros,* though Terence's riotous farce had been changed into a reflective tragedy, and once in *The Merchant of Yonkers,* though its principal personage did not appear in the Austrian prototype at all. The first of the credentials of my advisers in this matter, however, would be that they had decoded all six hundred pages of Joyce's crowded and mighty novel and realized how great were its differences from my three act comedy.

Sincerely yours,
Thornton Wilder

Washington, D.C.
December 17, 1942

More on Joyce

Why did Wilder admire Joyce and *Finnegans Wake* so deeply? These excerpts from a talk given at a meeting of the James Joyce Society in New York on February 2, 1954, offer clues. His subject was "Joyce and the Modern Novel."

First we would seek for our place in myths. Myths are the dreaming soul of the race, telling its story. Now, the dreaming soul of the race has told its story for centuries and centuries and centuries, and there have been billions of stories. They're still telling them. Every novel for sale in a railroad station is the dreaming soul of the human race telling its story. But the myths are the survival of the fittest of the billions of stories most of which have been forgotten. No chance survival there. The retelling of them on every hand occurs because they whisper a validation—they isolate and confer a significance—Prometheus, Cassandra, Oedipus, Don Quixote, Faust.

Joyce not only drew on myth; he used history as though it were myth. He made a hero who was Everyman, and to describe him to us he played on the vast repertory of myth and history as upon a clavier. . . .

The hero of *Finnegans Wake* is the most "generalized" character in all literature, but he is also completely a unique and individualized person. We overhear and oversee him in bed above his tavern at the edge of Dublin. His conscience is trying him for some obscure misdemeanors committed— or perhaps only partially envisaged—during the day. He is in disgrace. He identifies himself with Lucifer fallen from heaven, Adam ejected from Paradise, Napoleon defeated at Waterloo, Finnegan of the old ballot laid out for his wake. It is the Book of Falls, and as the night advances he plunges deeper and relives all the crimes of which man is capable; he stands trial (the very constellations of the night sky are sitting in judgment). He submits his defense and extenuation. Finally dawn arrives; the sun climbs through the transom of the Earwickers' bedroom. The last chapter is a wonderful sunburst of Handelian rhetoric; all the resurrection myths of the world are recalled along with Pears' soap advertisements and the passing trains and the milkman. The phoenix is reborn; Everyman re-awakes.

Wilder on Drama More Generally

Wilder completed the most extended statement of his views on the nature of drama, "Some Thoughts on Playwriting," just as he began writing *The Skin of Our Teeth*. (The statement was first published in 1941.) These two excerpts focus on "acting" and "pretense" in drama, for which *Skin* is a laboratory specimen.

[Fundamental Conditions]

Four fundamental conditions of the drama separate it from the other arts. Each of these conditions has its advantages and disadvantages, each requires a particular aptitude from the dramatist, and from each there are a number of instructive consequences to be derived. These conditions are:

   I. The theater is an art which reposes upon the work of many collaborators;

  II. It is addressed to the group-mind;

 III. It is based upon a pretense and its very nature calls out a multiplication of pretenses;

 IV. Its action takes place in a perpetual present time. . .

[The Actor As the Dramatist's Chief Collaborator]

The actor's gift is a combination of three separate faculties or endowments. Their presence to a high degree in any one person is extremely rare, although the ambition to possess them is common. Those who rise to the height of the profession represent a selection and a struggle for survival in one of the most difficult and cruel of the artistic activities. The three endowments that compose the gift are observation, imagination, and physical coordination:

  1. An observant and analyzing eye for all modes of behavior about us, for dress and manner, and for

the signs of thought and emotion in oneself and in
others.

2. The strength of imagination and memory whereby
the actor may, at the indication in the author's text,
explore his store of observations and represent the
details of appearance and the intensity of the emotions—joy, fear, surprise, grief, love, and hatred—
and through imagination extend them to intenser
degrees and to differing characterizations.

3. A physical coordination whereby the force of these
inner realizations may be communicated to voice,
face, and body.

An actor must *know* the appearances and the mental
states; he must *apply* his knowledge to the rôle; and he
must physically *express* his knowledge. Moreover, his con-
centration must be so great that he can effect this representation under conditions of peculiar difficulty—in abrupt
transition from the non-imaginative conditions behind
the stage; and in the presence of fellow actors who may
be momentarily destroying the reality of the action.

A dramatist prepares the characterization of his personages in such a way that it will take advantage of the actor's
gift.

Characterization in a novel is presented by the author's
dogmatic assertion that the personage was such, and by an
analysis of the personage with generally an account of his
or her past. Since in the drama this is replaced by the
actual presence of the personage before us and since there
is no occasion for the intervening all-knowing author to
instruct us as to his or her inner nature, a far greater share
is given in a play to (1) highly characteristic utterances and
(2) concrete occasions in which the character defines itself
under action and (3) a conscious preparation of the text

whereby the actor may build upon the suggestions in the rôle according to his own abilities.

Characterization in a play is like a blank check which the dramatist accords to the actor for him to fill in—not entirely blank, for a number of indications of individuality are already there, but to a far less definite and absolute degree than in the novel.

The dramatist's principal interest being the movement of the story, he is willing to resign the more detailed aspects of characterization to the actor and is often rewarded beyond his expectation.

The sleepwalking scene from *Macbeth* is a highly compressed selection of words whereby despair and remorse rise to the surface of indirect confession. It is to be assumed that had Shakespeare lived to see what the genius of Sarah Siddons could pour into the scene from that combination of observation, self-knowledge, imagination, and representational skill, even he might have exclaimed, "I never knew I wrote so well!"

[The Theater As Pretense]

It lives by conventions: a convention is an agreed-upon falsehood, a permitted lie.

Illustrations: Consider at the first performance of the *Medea,* the passage where Medea meditates the murder of her children. An anecdote from antiquity tells us that the audience was so moved by this passage that considerable disturbance took place.

The following conventions were involved:

1. Medea was played by a man.
2. He wore a large mask on his face. In the lip of the mask was an acoustical device for projecting the

voice. On his feet he wore shoes with soles and heels half a foot high.

3. His costume was so designed that it conveyed to the audience, by convention: woman of royal birth and Oriental origin.

4. The passage was in metric speech. All poetry is an "agreed-upon falsehood" in regard to speech.

5. The lines were sung in a kind of recitative. All opera involves this "permitted lie" in regard to speech.

Modern taste would say that the passage would convey much greater pathos if a woman "like Media" had delivered it—with an uncovered face that exhibited all the emotions she was undergoing. For the Greeks, however, there was no pretense that Medea was on the stage. The mask, the costume, the mode of declamation were a series of signs which the spectator interpreted and reassembled in his own mind. Medea was being re-created within the imagination of each of the spectators.

The history of the theater shows us that in its greatest ages the stage employed the greatest number of conventions. The stage is fundamental pretense and it thrives on the acceptance of that fact and in the multiplication of additional pretenses. When it tries to assert that the personages in the action "really are," really inhabit such-and-such rooms, really suffer such-and-such emotions, it loses rather than gains credibility. The modern world is inclined to laugh condescendingly at the fact that in the plays of Racine and Corneille the gods and heroes of antiquity were dressed like the courtiers under Louis XIV; that in the Elizabethan Age scenery was replaced by placards notifying the audience of the location; and that a whip in the hand and a jogging motion of the body indicated that a man was on horseback in the Chinese theater; these devices did not spring from naïveté, however, but from the vitality of the public imagination in those days and from an instinctive feeling as to where the essential and where the inessential lay in drama.

The convention has two functions:

1. It provokes the collaborative activity of the spectator's imagination; and
2. It raises the action from the specific to the general.

This second aspect is of even greater importance than the first.

If Juliet is represented as a girl "very like Juliet"—it was not merely a deference to contemporary prejudices that assigned this rôle to a boy in the Elizabethan Age— moving about in a "real" house with marble staircases, rugs, lamps, and furniture, the impression is irresistibly conveyed that these events happened to this one girl, in one place, at one moment in time. When the play is staged as Shakespeare intended it, the bareness of the stage releases the events from the particular and the experience of Juliet partakes of that of all girls in love, in every time, place, and language.

The stage continually strains to tell this generalized truth and it is the element of pretense that reinforces it. Out of the lie, the pretense, of the theater proceeds a truth more compelling than the novel can attain, for the novel by its own laws is constrained to tell of an action that "once happened"—"once upon a time."

The Skin of Our Teeth *on Broadway (1942–1943)*

Skin's original Playbill. Left to right: Sabina (Tallulah Bankhead), Mrs. Antrobus (Florence Eldridge), Mr. Antrobus (Fredric March), Gladys (Frances Heflin), George (Montgomery Clift).

At the opening of Act I, George Antrobus arrives home in Excelsior, New Jersey, carrying his latest discovery, the wheel. He is greeted by his adoring daughter, Gladys, and the lovable dinosaur and mammoth.

In Act II, the newly crowned Miss Atlantic City moves in on the recently elected president of the Ancient and Honorable Order of Mammals, Subdivision Humans.

At the end of Act II, George Antrobus leads his family to the ark and to safety. Behind him: Gladys, Henry, Mrs. Antrobus, and Sabina, with the Fortune Teller (Florence Reed) pointing and proclaiming, "They're safe. George Antrobus! Think it over! A new world to make—think it over!"

"I'm not afraid of you," Sabina (former camp follower) says to Henry (*the* former enemy) in Act III.

"In the beginning, God created the Heavens and the earth. . . ." Mr. Tremayne (Ralph Kellard), playing twelve o'clock, passes behind the Antrobuses, who are spending a quiet evening at home at the end of the play . . . and starting over once more.

Acknowledgments

The Afterword of this volume is constructed in large part from Thornton Wilder's words in unpublished letters, journals, business records, and publications not easy to come by. Readers interested in additional information about Thornton Wilder are referred to standard sources and to the Thornton Wilder Society's website: www.thorntonwildersociety.org.

Many Wilder fans deserve my thanks for helping me to accomplish this task, for which, of course, I bear full responsibility. Space permits me to extend thanks to only a few: Hugh Van Dusen, David Semanki, Barbara Whitepine, and Celeste Fellows. Four individuals deserve a special salute, and I am honored to give it: Barbara Hogenson, Paula Vogel, J. D. McClatchy, and Penelope Niven.

Letters and Journals

Quotations from Thornton Wilder's letters and his journal are taken from one of two principal sources: the unpublished letters, manuscripts, and related files in the Wilder Family Archives in the

Yale Collection of American Literature at the Beinecke Rare Book and Manuscript Library, and the Wilder family's own holdings, including many of Thornton Wilder's legal and agency papers. Minor spelling errors have been silently corrected. All rights are reserved for this material.

Publications

Excerpts from published sources are identified in the order of their appearance in the text, with permissions noted as required: Richard Maney's summary of *The Skin of Our Teeth* is printed in his memoir *Fanfare: The Confessions of a Press Agent* (New York: Harper & Row, 1957), p. 330. Copyright © 1957 by Richard Maney. Reprinted by permission of HarperCollins Publishers. The December 2, 1941, excerpt from Wilder's journal appears in Donald Gallup, Ed., *The Journals of Thornton Wilder, 1939–1961* (New Haven: Yale University Press, 1985), pp. 37–38. Copyright © 1985 by Union Trust Company. Reprinted by permission of Yale University Press. The excerpt from Wilder's "After a Visit to England" is published in *The Yale Review* XXXI: 2 (December 1941): 217–24. Reprinted courtesy of *The Yale Review*. Wilder's December 17, 1942, letter was published as "A Footnote to *The Skin of Our Teeth*," *The Yale Review* 87: 4 (October 1999): 68–70. Both *Yale Review* pieces are printed with the permission of Tappan Wilder.

On February 2, 1954, Wilder spoke to the James Joyce Society on "Joyce and the Modern Novel." He later adapted his lecture for publication by the James Joyce Society in 1957. It was published in Wilder's *American Characteristics & Other Essays* (New York: Harper & Row, 1957; Authors Guild Backinprint Edition, 2000), pp. 172–80. Reprinted by permission of Tappan Wilder. Wilder's "Some Thoughts on Playwrighting" first appeared in Augusto Centeno, Ed., *The Intent of the Artist*

(Princeton, N.J.: Princeton University Press, 1941) and is published in *American Characteristics & Other Essays,* pp. 115–26. Reprinted by permission of Tappan Wilder.

Photographs

The original 1942 cast Playbill is reproduced with the permission of PLAYBILL®. The five photographs of the original production appeared in *Life* magazine on November 30, 1942, pp. 93–100. They were taken by George Karger and reproduced with permission of George Karger/Pix Inc./Timepix. The author's photo, courtesy of the Yale Collection of American Literature and by permission of Tappan Wilder, shows Thornton Wilder playing the part of Mr. Antrobus in an unidentified summer stock production in 1947.

THORNTON WILDER

In his quiet way, Thornton Niven Wilder was a revolutionary writer who experimented boldly with literary forms and themes, from the beginning to the end of his long career. "Every novel is different from the others," he wrote when he was seventy-five. "The theater (ditto). . . . The thing I'm writing now is again totally unlike anything that preceded it." Wilder's richly diverse settings, characters, and themes are at once specific and global. Deeply immersed in classical as well as contemporary literature, he often fused the traditional and the modern in his novels and plays, all the while exploring the cosmic in the commonplace. In a January 12, 1953, cover story, *Time* took note of Wilder's unique "interplanetary mind"—his ability to write from a vision that was at once American and universal.

A pivotal figure in the history of twentieth-century letters, Wilder was a novelist and playwright whose works continue to be widely read and produced in this new century. He is the only writer to have won the Pulitzer Prize for both Fiction and Drama. His second novel, *The Bridge of San Luis Rey,* received the Fiction award in 1928, and he won the prize twice in Drama, for *Our Town* in 1938 and *The Skin of Our Teeth* in 1943. His other novels are *The Cabala, The Woman of Andros, Heaven's My Destination, The Ides of March, The Eighth Day,* and *Theophilus North.* His other major dramas include *The Matchmaker,* which was adapted as the internationally acclaimed musical comedy *Hello, Dolly!,* and *The Alcestiad.* Among his innovative shorter plays are *The Happy Journey to Trenton and Camden* and *The Long Christmas Dinner,* and two uniquely conceived series, *The Seven Ages of Man* and *The Seven Deadly Sins,* frequently performed by amateurs.

Wilder and his work received many honors, highlighted by the three Pulitzer Prizes, the Gold Medal for Fiction of the American Academy of Arts and Letters, the Order of Merit (Peru), the Goethe-Plakette der Stadt (Germany, 1959), the Presidential Medal of Freedom (1963), the National Book Committee's first National Medal for Literature (1965), and the National Book Award for Fiction (1967).

He was born in Madison, Wisconsin, on April 17, 1897, to Amos Parker Wilder and Isabella Niven Wilder. The family later lived in China and in California, where Wilder was graduated from Berkeley High School. After two years at Oberlin College, he went on to Yale, where he received his undergraduate degree in 1920. A valuable part of his education took place during summers spent working hard on farms in California, Kentucky, Vermont, Connecticut, and Massachusetts. His father arranged these rigorous "shirtsleeve" jobs for Wilder and his older brother, Amos, as part of their initiation into the American experience.

Thornton Wilder studied archaeology and Italian as a special student at the American Academy in Rome (1920–1921), and earned a master of arts degree in French literature at Princeton in 1926.

In addition to his talents as playwright and novelist, Wilder was an accomplished teacher, essayist, translator, scholar, lecturer, librettist, and screenwriter. In 1942, he teamed with Alfred Hitchcock to write the first draft of the screenplay for the classic thriller *Shadow of a Doubt*, receiving credit as principal writer and a special screen credit for his "contribution to the preparation" of the production. All but fluent in four languages, Wilder translated and adapted plays by such varied authors as Henrik Ibsen, Jean-Paul Sartre, and André Obey. As a scholar, he conducted significant research on James Joyce's *Finnegans Wake* and the plays of Spanish dramatist Lope de Vega.

Wilder's friends included a broad spectrum of figures on both sides of the Atlantic—Hemingway, Fitzgerald, Alexander Woollcott, Gene Tunney, Sigmund Freud, producer Max Reinhardt, Katharine Cornell, Ruth Gordon and Garson Kanin. Beginning in the mid-1930s, Wilder was especially close to Gertrude Stein and became one of her most effective interpreters and champions. Many of Wilder's friendships are documented in his prolific correspondence. Wilder believed that great letters constitute a "great branch of literature." In a lecture entitled "On Reading the Great Letter Writers," he wrote that a letter can function as a "literary exercise," the "profile of a personality," and "news of the soul," apt descriptions of thousands of letters he wrote to his own friends and family.

Wilder enjoyed acting and played major roles in several of his own plays in summer theater productions. He also possessed a lifelong love of music: reading musical scores was a hobby, and he wrote the librettos for two operas based on his work: *The Long Christmas Dinner*, with composer Paul Hindemith; and *The Alcestiad*, with composer Louise Talma. Both works premiered in Germany.

Teaching was one of Wilder's deepest passions. He began his teaching career in 1921 as an instructor in French at Lawrenceville, a private secondary school in New Jersey. Financial independence after the publication of *The Bridge of San Luis Rey* permitted him to leave the classroom in 1928, but he returned to teaching in the 1930s at the University of Chicago. For six years, on a part-time basis, he taught courses there in classics in translation, comparative literature, and composition. In 1950–1951, he served as the Charles Eliot Norton Professor of Poetry at Harvard. Wilder's gifts for scholarship and teaching (he treated the classroom as all but a theater) made him a consummate, much-sought-after lecturer in his own country and abroad. After World War II, he held special standing, especially in Germany, as an interpreter of his own country's intellectual traditions and their influence on cultural expression.

During World War I, Wilder had served a three-month stint as an enlisted man in the Coast Artillery section of the army, stationed at Fort Adams, Rhode Island. He volunteered for service in World War II, advancing to the rank of lieutenant colonel in Army Air Force Intelligence. For his service in North Africa and Italy, he was awarded the Legion of Merit, the Bronze Star, the Chevalier Legion d'Honneur, and honorary officership in the Military Order of the British Empire (M.B.E.).

From royalties received from *The Bridge of San Luis Rey*, Wilder built a house for his family in 1930 in Hamden, Connecticut, just outside New Haven. But he typically spent as many as two hundred days a year away from Hamden, traveling to and settling in a variety of places that provided the stimulation and solitude he needed for his work. Sometimes his destination was the Arizona desert, the MacDowell Colony in New Hampshire, or Martha's Vineyard, Newport, Saratoga, Vienna, or Baden-Baden. He wrote aboard ships, and often chose to stay in "spas in off-season." He needed a certain refuge when he was deeply immersed in writing a novel or play. Wilder explained his habit to a *New Yorker* journalist in 1959: "The walks, the quiet—all the elegance is present, everything is there but the people. That's it! A spa in off-season! I make a practice of it."

But Wilder always returned to "the house *The Bridge* built," as it is still known to this day. He died there of a heart attack on December 7, 1975.

■ Perennial

THE IDES OF MARCH
ISBN 0-06-008890-7 (paperback)
With a new Foreword by Kurt Vonnegut, Jr.

First published in 1948, *The Ides of March* is a brilliant epistolary novel of Julius Caesar's Rome. Through imaginary letters and documents, Wilder brings to life a dramatic period of world history and one of its magnetic personalities.

"What distinguishes [*The Ides of March*] is a rich, shrewd, and glowing characterization of Caesar's restless mind." —*New York Times*

THE EIGHTH DAY
ISBN 0-06-008891-5 (paperback)
With a new Foreword by John Updike

First published in 1967, near the end of Wilder's life, this novel moves back and forth through the 20th century, telling the story of a talented inventor accused of murder.

PLAYS

THREE PLAYS
Our Town, The Skin of Our Teeth, and *The Matchmaker*
ISBN 0-06-051264-4 (Perennial Classics paperback)
With a new Foreword by John Guare

This omnibus volume brings together the definitive texts of three outstanding plays by one of America's most distinguished writers.

OUR TOWN: *A Play*
ISBN 0-06-051263-6 (Perennial Classics paperback)
With a new Foreword by Donald Margulies

First produced and published in 1938, this Pulitzer Prize–winning drama of life in the small village of Grover's Corners has become an American classic and is Thornton Wilder's most renowned and most frequently performed play.

"Mr. Wilder has transmuted the simple events of human life into universal reverie. . . . One of the finest achievements of the current stage." —Brooks Atkinson

THE SKIN OF OUR TEETH: *A Play*
ISBN 0-06-008893-1 (Perennial Classics paperback)
With a new Foreword by Paula Vogel

Wilder's Pulitzer Prize–winning (1943) madcap comedy of how the Antrobus family and its maid prevail over successive catastrophes has become a timeless statement about human endurance and hope . . . and the imperishable vitality of theater.

"It is not easy to think of any other American play with so good a chance of being acted a hundred years from now." —Alexander Woollcott, *Atlantic Monthly,* 1944

Available wherever books are sold, or call 1-800-331-3761 to order.

Perennial is proud to reissue the works of Thornton Wilder. Each has a new Foreword by a noted writer, as well as new documentary material edited by Tappan Wilder.

NOVELS

THE BRIDGE OF SAN LUIS REY

ISBN 0-06-008887-7 (Perennial Classics paperback)
With a new Foreword by Russell Banks

The Bridge of San Luis Rey opens in the aftermath of an inexplicable tragedy—a footbridge in Peru breaks and five people fall to their deaths. For Brother Juniper, a humble monk who witnesses the catastrophe, the question is inescapable: why those five? Through the device of Brother Juniper's drive to understand whether their deaths were caused by fate or divine intervention, Wilder's 1928 Pulitzer Prize–winning novel explores what is important and what is lasting about life and living.

"One of the greatest reading novels in this century's American writing." —Edmund Fuller

THEOPHILUS NORTH

ISBN 0-06-008892-3 (paperback)
With a new Foreword by Christopher Buckley

An exhausted 29-year-old teacher arrives in Newport, Rhode Island, in the summer of 1926. To support himself, he takes jobs in the great homes of families living along Ocean Drive—playing the roles of tutor, spy, confidante, lover, friend, and enemy in the colorful, tension-filled upstairs-and-downstairs world of Newport in the golden 1920s. Along the way, the novel raises gentle but trenchant questions about what's important, the nature and role of youth, and what wealth does to those who have it and those who do not.

"A testimony to the human race." —*New York Times Book Review*

HEAVEN'S MY DESTINATION

ISBN 0-06-008889-3 (paperback)
With a new Foreword by J. D. McClatchy

First published in 1934, *Heaven's My Destination* contains one of Wilder's most memorable characters: the heroic traveling textbook salesman George Marvin Brush. George's territory is the Midwest and, as a fervent religious convert, he is determined to lead a good Christian life. But his travels take him through smoking cars, bawdy houses, and trailer camps of Depression-era America with often hilarious results.

"A good sardonic etching of this most godless of American ages." —*Commonweal*

THE CABALA AND THE WOMAN OF ANDROS

ISBN 0-06-051857-X (paperback)
With a new Foreword

Two of Wilder's early novels are collected here: *The Cabala* (1926), a fantasy about American expatriates, and *The Woman of Andros* (1930), a novel in which Wilder creates a character that serves as his archetype of the virtue of hope.